Mysteriously Speaking . . .

Don Miller's copy of TMF 6:2 was returned to me by the
postal service marked "Deceased." Many of TMF's subscribers
knew Don through his various mystery fanzines, the most sig-
nificant of which was *The Mystery Nook*, which Don intended to
be a quarterly but which his poor health kept him from putting
out at other than irregular intervals. Some of you knew Don
much better than I did. I actually saw him only twice. Once,
in the mid-seventies, when I was in Washington for a convention
I really didn't want to attend, I escaped out to Don's house in
Wheaton for a long, leisurely Saturday of prowling through his
basement full of books (this was before he sold most of them to
Howard Waterhouse [who is now also deceased]) and sitting around
and talking in the upstairs room from which he conducted his
fan activities. While there I also met his wife, son, daughter,
and oversized dog, all of whom were most pleasant and regarded
with amused tolerance the enthusiasm we two grown men showed
for playing with books and amateur magazines.
     The second time I saw him was at the Bouchercon in Washing-
ton two years ago. Don had cancer and, I think, other health
problems, and he looked thinner and more drawn than I remembered. He was quite cheerful, though, and gave no hint that
things were going badly for him. Indeed, that he was up and
about at all quite astonished me, because his health in the
previous year had been so bad that he had had to drop out of
the Stout bibliographical project on which we were working.
Originally, *Rex Stout: An Annotated Primary and Secondary Bibliography* was to have been the work of Don Miller, John McAleer,
Arriean Schemer, and myself, but Don became so ill when the
project was just beginning to get under way that he witdrew.
Even so, his Rex Stout Memorial Issue of *The Mystery Nook*,
which had come out several years earlier, was of incalculable
help to us in completing the *Bibliography*, so Don was a con-
tributor to that volume, albeit before the fact. Don's with-
drawal made it possible for us to add Jud Sapp's name to the
title page as the fourth editor. Jud's name should have been
there to start with, as his contribution was at least as great
as that of any of the other editors, and Don's gracious with-
drawal enabled us to correct that error. But Don's name appeared in the book after all, in larger letters than any of
ours, because we dedicated *Rex Stout*, as I am dedicating this
issue of TMF,

To Don Miller
who would have been with us if he could

†

Rather to my surprise, two dozen TMFers have written to say
that they would purchase reprints of the first seven issues of
TMF at $20 for the set, so I'll get to work on that project as
soon as this issue is out of the way. Those of you who have
already said you'd buy the set may wait, if you wish, until the
books arrive in your mailbox before sending payment. (They
should be ready within a month of when you receive TMF 6:3.)
Anyone else wanting a set should send me a check for $20.00.
    Speaking of buying books by mail, you should know, if you
don't already, that Bob and Phyllis Weinberg (15145 Oxford Dr.,
Oak Forest, IL 60452) put out a splendid list of *new* books and
such every month. If you live next door to a mystery specialty
book shop, the Weinberg's twenty-page lists won't be of much
value to you; otherwise, they will be. The lists aren't just
for mystery fans. Science fiction, fantasy, horror, comics,
and the pulps are also covered, but Bob and Phyllis have a good
eye for what is likely to interest the mystery fan. The June
catalogue, for example, offers Bill Pronzini's latest, *Scatter-
shot*, at $10.95, with a label signed by Pronzini laid in at no
extra cost. They are also strong on analytical works, so if
you are now, or are likely to be in the future, in the market
for new books in, or about the mystery genre, you ought to be on
the Weinbergs' mailing list.
    I also recently received mystery catalogue #17 from Waves
Press and Bookshop (4040 MacArthur Ave., Richmond, VA 23227).
Used books for the serious collector. The highest price I saw
in a quick glance through the nine pages of listings was $95,
and a large proportion of the offerings fell into the $5-$10
range.
    Long-time subscribers to TMF know that my favorite cata-
logues are those put out by Enola Stewart's Gravesend Books
(Box 235, Pocono Pines, PA 18350), and I am pleased to say
that catalogue 27 is now in print. If you don't have it yet,
you're probably not on Enola's list, but you can get a copy by
sending her $5. *What?--I* heard someone say--*Me pay some book
dealer five bucks just to tell me what she has for sale? Not
on your life!* Well, calm down and listen. Gravesend Books
catalogues are not just listings of books for sale; they are
valuable reference books in their own right. And the $5 they
sell for probably doesn't do much more than cover the cost of
production. What we are talking about is not a collection of
smudgy, mimeographed pages carelessly stapled together. What
we are talking about is a beautifully produced, 6" x 9",
sixty-four page, saddle-stapled booklet, typeset and printed
on fine (and damned expensive) coated stock throughout. As
for the contents, all of the entries are annotated and the
prices, while they may be a bit disturbing to those of us who
do most of our book-buying in Good Will stores, are about par
for the big leagues. Serious collectors quite literally can't
afford to do without this catalogue as a catalogue, and the
rest of us will find it extremely useful as a reference.
    Paperback Quarterly (1710 Vincent, Brownwood, TX 76801)
is making a mighty effort to get back on schedule after falling

victim to the lateness malady that sooner or later afflicts all
amateur and semi-pro magazines (some of us it afflicts both
sooner *and* later). The Winter 1981 issue arrived a short time
ago, and boy is it a beauty. Laid in on page 27 is a lovely,
lovely, full-color photograph of four paperback covers featuring skeletons. (The article accompanying the photo is by that
well-known Howdy Doody lookalike, Bill Crider.) And if that
isn't enough to set your heart to pounding, page 31 features a
laid-in facsimile of one of those cut-out covers that have become popular of late--and PQ's facsimile is itself cut out! No
challenge is apparently too great for Editor Billy Lee and his
peerless crew. Subs are $10 per year ($15 overseas), and single
issues can be had for $3.50 each.

Skullduggery, the semi-pro mystery fiction magazine, has
died and been resurrected as Spiderweb. Most of you recall
that the original Skullduggery was the creation of Mike Cook,
who edited it for a year or so before turning it over to Karen
Shapiro, Bill Desmond, and Will Murray. A second shakeup has
since taken place, and Karen and Bill are now carrying on alone.
To distinguish their new effort from what had gone before, they
decided to rename their publication, so with the Winter 1982
issue Skullduggery became Spiderweb. Inside the covers, however, things remain pretty much the same, and that's a good
thing. Spiderweb provides a place for new writers to break in
to print, and that's desperately needed in today's shrunken
literary marketplace. Maybe the stories in Spiderweb won't win
many Edgars, but they are still good reading, and if you are
looking for a way to support and encourage aspiring new writers
in the mystery field you could do a lot worse than to subscribe
to Spiderweb. The quarterly issues are $2.50 each, and a year's
subscription is $10. The address is Drawer F, MIT Branch Sta-
tion, Cambridge, MA 02139.

Rober Martin (1, route d'Halanzy, Piedmont, 54350 Mont-
Saint-Martin, FRANCE) has begun a magazine called Hard Boiled
Dicks devoted to American hard-boiled detective writers. It
occurs to me as I type this that I haven't the faintest idea
how much Roger charges for American subscriptions (we swap
subs, you see, so no money changes hands), and that's too bad
because I think a lot of you, if you have any command of the
French language, are going to want to subscribe to HBD. The
magazine is roughly the same size and format as TMF, but its
contents are typeset and Roger makes liberal use of photos and
cover art. HBD #1 (November 1981) was devoted entirely to
Marvin H. Albert, whose pseudonyms include Mike Barone, Albert
Conroy, Anthony Rome, Ian MacAlister, and Nick Quarry. HBD #2
(March 1982) featured Michael Collins, whose real name, of
course, is Dennis Lynds and who has also written under the
names Mark Sadler, Carl Dekker, John Douglas, William Arden,
and John Crowe. HBD #3, scheduled for June 1982, will be devoted to William Campbell Gault. Roger's original intent was
to devote each issue of HBD to a single author, but he seems
to have changed his mind on this, since HBD #4 (due out in
September or October) will be devoted to three authors--Joseph
Hansen, Elmore Leonard, and Joe L. Hensley. The two issues I
have in my possession are extremely useful, containing exten-
sive biographical and bibliographical information. If you have
no French whatever, you won't get much out of HBD, but even
high-school French should enable you to make use of this valuable publication, and I urge you to support Roger's work by

subscribing to HBD. Perhaps, Roger, you can pass along the
subscription rates for foreign subscribers?
   Those of you who don't read French may be gnashing your
teeth over the knowledge that these things exist but you can't
read them, and I know how you feel. For years I have suffered
similar feelings every time a new issue of Iwan Hedman's DAST
showed up in the mailbox. Now those feelings are compounded
greatly by the realization that another Scandinavian--Bjarne
Nielsen by name--is happily putting out mystery fan publica-
tions--in Danish, this time. There's not a chance in hell--
less than that, really--that I'll ever learn Danish, yet I hold
in my hand three copies of a fanzine entitled *Pinkerton*, and
one of the issues leads off with an article on Nero Wolfe! Why
on earth did our ancestors have to mess around with that bloody
tower, anyway? If any of you are interested in subscribing,
the annual cost of this quarterly publication is $8, and you
should send your check to *Pinkerton*, Tidsskrift om Spaendings-
litteratur, Antikvariat Pinkerton, Nansensgade 68, 1366 Køben-
havn K, DANMARK. Also available from the same place is *Sherlock Holmes I Danmark*, a twenty-page booklet which appears to
be a bibliography of the Master's appearances in the Danish
language. The price is $4. For $3 you can also purchase a
sixteen-page booklet entitled *A Case of Identity* by Anders
Fage-Pedersen. This is an English translation (by Bjarne Nielsen) of Fage-Pedersen's 1963 *Sherlockiana* article which answered
the two questions of what happened to Holmes when he dropped
out of sight from 1891 to 1894 and why he is apparently im-
mortal. ("I shall prove that Sherlock under the alias Dr.
Nikola in the year 1892 forced his way into the holy lama
monastery in Tibet and there from the Tibetan monks he learned
the secret of their experiments in immortality--experiments
which at the time were not complete, but which Holmes was later
to complete successfully.") And finally, there is a 132-page
paperbound book by Bjarne Nielsen entitled *Hvem Begik Hvad?
Dansk Kriminallitteratur Indtil 1979: En Bibliografi*. It
doesn't require any knowledge of Danish to figure out that this
is a bibliography of Danish crime fiction, and a glance through
the pages confirms that the bibliography is exclusively Danish
--or, at least, that there are no English, American, or French
authors cited. I can't say about German, Norwegian, or Swedish
authors, since I can't distinguish them from Danish names.
Anyway, Nielsen is selling this bibliography for $15.
   Though this issue of TMF will arrive too late for this news
to be timely, I pass along the following news release for the
information of the readership at large and specifically for
those who might be interested in participating in future activities of The Maltese Falcon Society.
   The New York Chapter of the Maltese Falcon Society announces its
   first Annual Dashiell Hammett Walking Tour for Saturday, June 26,
   1982. This one-mile tour in search of Hammett's life in New York
   City during the 1930's features visits to various Hammett residences,
   such as where the master mystery writer created the characters of
   Nick and Nora Charles, and where he wrote some of his Sam Spade
   short stories. Also visited will be the home of *Black Mask* Magazine,
   the pulp that began the American hard-boiled tradition in mystery
   stories, as well as the site of Hammett's original publishers. Anecdotes will be recounted throughout this tour, placing the sites visited in their proper perspective in the life of the hard-boiled
   fiction master.

(Continued on page 26)

Spy Series Characters in Hardback Part XII

By Barry Van Tilburg

DOSSIER #60: Bernard Newman and Francis (Papa) Pontivy.
CREATED BY: Bernard Newman.
OCCUPATION: Newman worked for British Intelligence before be-
coming an assistant and friend to Papa Pontivy, Head of
Counterespionage for the Surete and the Duxieme Bureau.
When France was invaded by the Nazis, he escaped to Eng-
land with the help of Newman to continue the fight against
the Nazi spies. Later, because of age and their knowledge
of spies and their activities, they both become consultants
for Scotland Yard and the Surete.
ASSOCIATES: Inspector Marshall, their friend at Scotland Yard;
George Delamere, a reformed burglar and safe cracker who
often helps them out.
WEAPONS: Both use revolvers.
OTHER COMMENTS: Newman writes the memoirs of Pontivy as Watson
did for Sherlock Holmes. Newman describes Pontivy as a
very good likeness of Agatha Christie's Hercule Poirot.
Instead of referring to his "grey cells" as Poirot did,
Pontivy refers to his instincts to finds his man and then
proceeds to develop evidence against him. He is a master
detective. That is what counterespionage work is--the
detecting of a person or persons who are carrying out
criminal activities against another country or countries.

Spy (Gollancz, 1935).
Secret Servant (Gollancz, 1935).
The Mussolini Murder Plot (Gollancz, 1936; Hillman-Curl, 1939).
Death Under Gibraltar (Gollancz, 1938).
The Maginot Line Murder (Gollancz, 1939).
Death to the Spy (Gollancz, 1939).
Siegfried Spy (Gollancz, 1939).
Death to the Fifth Column (Gollancz, 1941).
Secret Weapon (Gollancz, 1942).
Black Market (Gollancz, 1942).
Second Front--First Spy (Gollancz, 1944).
Spy Catchers (Gollancz, 1945).
The Spy in the Brown Derby (Gollancz, 1945).
They Saved London (Gollancz, 1946).
Dead Man Murder (Gollancz, 1946).
Moscow Murder (Gollancz, 1948).
The Flying Saucer (Gollancz, 1948).
Cup Final Murder (Gollancz, 1950).

(Continued on page 26)

(By Frank Hamilton)

Pirates in Candyland

By Bob Sampson

Not many pulp magazines featured a lead female criminal. Plenty of crooked ladies appeared in pulp fiction, but few of these realized that special glory of their own series.

Most usually, girls were written in to decorate the prose and to get tied up and rescued. For a maiden in distress is one thing, but a maiden with a revolver who steals your wallet is quite another.

In the history of the pulps, lead female criminals came in two bursts. The first group arrived early in the adolescence of the pulp magazine; the second batch appeared during the mid-1930's. There were not many of either.

Through 1918, *Detective Story Magazine* featured a brief series about Boston Betty, a tricky young thief, and her clever fox terrier, Alibi. Soon after this, probably during the early 1920's, Edgar Wallace published the adventures of Four-Square Jane in English periodicals as yet unidentified. During 1927, a blonde whiz named Pat the Piper appeared in an uneven short story series in *Flynn's*.

In the mid-1930's, a group of reprehensible women appeared en masse in the magazine *Scarlet Adventuress*, whose bright purple and scarlet fiction, snorting with sex, featured crooked harlots and wantons. These demonstrated to male readers how much fun it was to be liberated women. On a less fleshy plane, Vivian Legrande, The Lady From Hell, was featured in a 21-story series that ran in *Detective Fiction Weekly* during 1935-1936.

Of these, Boston Betty was humdrum and Pat the Piper trivial. Four-Square Jane was wonderfully resourceful, although she was less a crook than a law-abiding girl forced to steal back her own fortune. The Lady From Hell is a splendid, cold-hearted, murdering, scheming, wicked wench of high originality and force.

Aside from these splendid examples of feminine resolution, one other female criminal deserves recognition. She was neither trivial nor humdrum, and she was most certainly not law-abiding. She was, no less, a pirate, an attractive lone wolf working out a permanent grudge against society.

Her name was Blue Jean Billy and her haunts were the *Detective Story Magazine*, off the New England coast.

Her hair was a wavy chestnut ...; there was a flush of a healthy tan on her face and consequent faint border lines on her throat and forearm ...; her eyes were gray, and they could be very soft

7

or very hard in a shifting flash; her body was strong and lithe, every move gave hint of steely muscles, of perfect synchronism; each movement was timed, and there was no lost motion.

One thing was stamped on her. She was bred to the great outdoors.... She was about the swellest bit of feminine loveliness that [the guard] had seen in a long time.... A sudden soft movement that had come to him out of the corner of his eye.... Detective Gillane was looking straight into the business end of an automatic gat.... Her whole being had undergone a swift and almost unbelievable change. Warmth and sunshine were at once transmuted into blued steel. When next she spoke, her words were snapped off in short, crude phrasings:

"Stick 'em up!" ("Raggedy Ann," Chapter III.)

The adorable young lady who turns to metal is Miss Blue Jean Billy Race--a curious name that has nothing to do with the style pants she wore. "Blue" for the ocean and "Jean" for the gracious gift of God. The rest was her father's name, old William J. Race, old Quality Bill.

By profession, Billy is that unique thing--a pirate, a "Highway Woman of the Sea," as the author archly remarks. At the beginning of the series in *Detective Story Magazine*, her attention is more often on shore. But within a few issues, the action veers out toward the brine and salty to her prime targets--the yachts of rich men, the bloated arrogant kind, puffing $2 cigars as they brag fatly of how they skinned widows' and crippled children.

It is night. Over the yacht railing glides a slender figure dressed in black--Blue Jean Billy in full war attire. She pads to the main cabin. There revel the forces of evil: the exclusive party well washed by bootleg fluids; the card game rigged to trim the sucker. Here jewels glitter around wealthy necks and wallets swell fat with gold backs, perhaps honestly come by but probably not.

The door clicks open. The muzzle of the heavy automatic circles and the girl, standing taut, surveys her catch, her brown eyes iced, contemptuous, chilling as the moving muzzle.

Protests shiver up. What giant of industry wishes to bend submissively to a slender bit of a girl? It's indecent; unmanly, even.

A buxom little thing, at that. Hardly 100 pounds. She is soaking wet, dressed only in a simple swimming suit, her 1918 ankles immodestly revealed.

Let the red-faced captain of industry protest too much and gun-sound splits his words. The table top rips with bullet impact. Usually that quells them. The red faces shine wetly. It's terrifying--a crazy woman--no lady shoots in the presence of a gentleman.

No lady talks to a gentleman as she does, either.

She begins the proceeding with a long speech. It looks good on paper, but, since it runs almost a column long, we may suppose that Mr. Tyler, author of the series, has enlarged and expanded her comments. These are concerned with the disagreeably low morals of those under her gun. How unworthy they are; what intolerable liars and cheats they are.

The purpose of such lectures is to lend a high literary tone to a hold-up. Why, she's a benefactor of humanity to rob these cultured scum. After several stories, Billy will give up this sermonizing and just as well. It reminds you of the pious

remarks Jesse James would make before cleaning out the bank.
You know what kind of an end he came to.
    Mr. Tyler rather sweats to justify Billy's activities in
terms of an avenging administrator of justice. He can't do
it. True, she preys on crooks and near crooks, but her trade
is piracy and grand larceny, for all that.
    Now back to the robbery. Once pockets are emptied and
necks stripped bare, the swag is wrapped in a rubber bag.
Silently, Blue Jean slips back into the night. On deck, she
stuffs the pistol into a waterproof pouch worn low at her
waist.
    Thus disarmed, she is at once vulnerable. A dozen men,
flushing with belated courage, drive at her. But too late.
Already she is over the railing. They hear her splash into the
black water. Then silence.
    Occasionally, for variety's sake, there is a chase, search
lights jabbing about, motorized launches butting among the
waves. Once, twice, there are gunfights out on the face of the
ocean--orange flashes at wave bases, the boats pitching, the
heaving black surface concealing that adroit swimmer. Silent
as light, she slips along wave troughs to a distant fishing
boat, and so away.
    The pound of a two-cycle engine recedes in the night....
    Charles W. Tyler wrote the series--one of several series he
provided for *Detective Story Magazine*. Tyler was born in Cleveland, Ohio, in 1848. After graduation from Kenyon College he
became a newspaper man, first working on the *Cleveland Leader*
and then, in 1885, joining the *Sun* staff in New York City.
During the First World War, he was associated with *Harvey's
Weekly* and provided editorials for both the *Sun* and the *Herald
Tribune*. He published pulp fiction in the general magazines of
the period, including *Railroad Man's Magazine* and *People's Magazine*, as well as *Detective Story Magazine*. In 1923, after a
brief illness, he died at his home in Point Pleasant, New Jersey.
    The Blue Jean Billy stories are less a series than a loosely-
linked collection of novelettes. They run chronologically with
vast time breaks between, each threatening to be the last. From
1918 to 1931, eleven stories appeared in *Detective Story Magazine*.
    Just how it was possible for an author who died in 1923 to
publish new novelettes in 1925, 1926, 1930, and 1931 is not
easily explained. It seems to be an outstanding instance of
ghost writing. Since Tyler's Big Nose Charlie series (about an
amiable old crook) also continued through the 1920's we conclude:
    --that Tyler's name was retained while others continued the
    series, or
    --that an immense store of Tyler manuscripts existed at the
    time of his death, or
    --that the Charles W. Tyler identified in the preceding
    paragraphs was not, after all, the Charles W. Tyler who
    wrote the Blue Jean Billy series.
This commentator regrets that he is able to shed only darkness
on this problem and appeals to others who might be able to explain matters.
    Whoever wrote what and when, Billy was popular enough for
her adventures to be published in two Chelsea House hardbacks:
Quality Bill's Girl (1925) and *Blue Jean Billy* (1926). These
books consisted of novelettes which had been published in *De-*

tective Story Magazine; the beginning and ending of each novel-
ette was editorially mangled to provide a little continuity and
give the illusion that each book was a novel.
   Billy's career begins with some spectacular crimes. The
initial story, "Raggedy Ann" (March 26, 1918)--the name refers
to an island out in the Atlantic off the Massachusetts coast--
tells how she held up the fancy engagement party. Not only
does she glom all the expensive presents, but she kidnaps the
groom, who rejoices in the name Algernon Whosis Pinagree Smythe.
   Because of this crime, the celebrated detective Robert Wood
sets out on Billy's trail. In "Raiders from Raggedy Ann" (July
16, 1918), she saves Wood's neck and foils a pack of crooks
with political connections. Now Billy invests part of the
stolen proceeds in the "Nix's Mate" (March 11, 1919), a shabby
boat with a souped-up engine. The rest of the loot she spends
on a few fancy dresses and the purchase of a society gambling
house.
   Once this place is packed with jeweled women and florid
men, Billy and her father's old friend, the Shanghai Kid, hold
up the whole crowd, clean them out, and away they go through a
secret tunnel, barely evading the police. After a violent encounter with a gang of wharf thugs, they escape to sea.
   But the crooks come snuffling her out. In "The Haunt of
Raggedy Ann" (October 7, 1919), one harsh event follows another,
including a full-scale gun fight. The *Nix's Mate* sinks and
Shanghai is killed. Billy and Wood, tightly trussed, are im-
prisoned aboard a beached wreck captained by a crazy man. At
this very moment, a furious storm breaks, just when it's most
needed. The crooks die in the sea. Billy reforms and marries
Wood, who retires from the detective trade to become a lobster-
man.
   How a sweet young buxom girl got into all this hurrah makes
a surprising story. It seems that her father, William J. Race,
old Quality Bill, was arrested by error and crippled by a
police third degree. Raging, he turned to a life of crime,
hating society and all its frauds. His daughter, Billy, was
brought up in his path--although he came to doubt that he had
done the wise thing.
   He died, leaving Billy an old brick house at 19 Green
Street (city not specified) and a shanty, where Billy had been
born, located out on Fiddler's Elbow, a sand spit angled very
far into the Atlantic. He also left her with an abiding con-
tempt for liars, cheats, double dealers, and those who use
wealth and social position to sock it to their neighbors.
   Three family friends were entrusted to keep an eye on Billy
as she grew up. It was a deadly assignment. Shaver Michael
died standing off the wharf rats in "Raggedy Ann." The Shanghai
Kid died in a hail of gun fire in "The Haunt of Raggedy Ann."
So far as is known, the third friend, the tough, old, one-handed
Kil Van Kull, lasted the course, although the law was hot after
him for months.
   All this history of crippled hopes is provided to justify
Billy's violently anti-social activities. To emphasize that
she does right by doing wrong, strong social distortions are
written into the narrative. Thus the rich folks Billy robs are
uniformly corrupt and venial, using their high positions to
ignore the law. Obviously, such people are born to be robbed;
it's only just that they be punished. So Billy, the Highway
Woman, joins that distinguished group of characters who worked

outside the law to punish those the law could not touch--a
group including The Three Just Men, Bulldog Drummond, and the
Spider.

The ruthless distortions used to characterize Billy's victims are also applied to her opponents. These are of three
kinds: lawmen of transcendent goodness who perceive her excel-
lence and forgive her actions; lawmen of corrupt cruelty,
simple as a rubber stamp; and, finally, faceless thugs, wharf
rats, cut-throats, sneaks, and assorted waterfront scum whose
one-dimensional qualities add menace without fatiguing the
reader.

The June 25, 1921, story, "Blue Jean Billy at Fiddler's
Reach," picks up after a three-year gap in narrative time. At
once, Bob Wood falls victim to the curse hovering over the
spouses of pulp-series characters--he gets drowned in Chapter
One. While Billy seeks to revive him, she is recognized by the
ferocious detective, Jerome Birwell, one of those baaaad lawmen.

He just misses capturing her, but his brutal ways hurl her
back to crime.

Away we go once more. In both "Blue Jean Billy at Fiddler's
Reach" and "Highway Woman of the Sea" (August 19, 1922), she
holds up boats, gets chased by Birwell and his horde of dock
scum. She makes them look foolish. During the activities of
"Highway Woman of the Sea," she gets hit on the head and cap-
tured. But not to worry. She escapes and rescues the whole-
some good police captain and his wife. The story ends in a
scene requiring two hankies or a small thick towel.

Now a two-and-a-half-year pause. Tyler dies; *Detective
Story Magazine* continues; and readers wonder whatever happened
to Billy. The best guess seems to be that the series is picked
up again and continued under Tyler's name by hands unknown.
It begins in the April 4, 1925, issue, "Blue Jean Billy, Sky
Pirate," describing how she uses a hydroplane to rob a private
boat. On that boat, a naughty fellow is tricking foolish fel-
lows with crooked cards. Billy arrives with gun and departs
carrying all the money and the signed card deck. The crooks,
desperate to get back the evidence, hire a detective to locate
her.

He does so by aerial reconnaissance. Before you know it,
Fiddler's Reach is again invaded by a snarling gang of cut-
throats. The good-guy detective gets somewhat shot, but Billy
is able to save the day without his assistance.

In "Blue Jean Billy and the Lone Survivor" (August 22,
1925), still another gang of thugs kills Old Lobster Joe. They
lay the blame on Billy, but she settles their hash. The November 6, 1926, "Blue Jean Billy, Waif of the Sea," features the
ultimate, last, final invasion of Fiddler's Reach. This time
Billy is falsely accused of bank robbery and murder. Clearing
herself, if barely, she decides to cut all ties with the past.
She fires the Fiddler's Reach establishment and leaves forever,
amid cascades of pathetic adjectives. Renaming herself Arlin
Shores, Billy becomes the resident guest of the Peasleys--
Captain Lige and Aunt Sophy.

For a year, it's quiet and peace. It's happiness days at
the Peasley's, all warm and sunny and glad and described in
prose concocted from sugar paste. It is pure slush, sentiment
run mad, affecting even locale names, which appear to have been
lifted from a copy of Raggedy Ann and Andy in Candyland:

[The] lapping of tiny waves on the pebbly shore of Blue Gingham
Bay. Distant surf breaking on Shabby Rocks.... The lazy clang
of the bell off Pumpkin Knob.... And a light shining from the
window of a big rambling while house in Calico Lane. (From
"Blue Jean Billy Plays Fair," January 18, 1930.)

No mistake about it--we're in Candyland.
Both "Blue Jean Billy Plays Fair" and "Sea Law and Blue
Jean Billy" (November 14, 1931) use essentially the same theme.
As Arlin Shores, Billy saves some incautious teen-agers from
rum-running gangsters. In the process her real identity is
discovered--and ignored by the people she helps.
By this late date, the story menace is no longer a tough
dick or a batch of wharf rats but sure-enough Al Capone gangsters, complete with sneers and pin-striped machine guns.
"Plays Fair" ends in a gun fight during which Billy kills her
first and last thug. In "Sea Law," she rescues the fool girl,
hijacks the bootleggers' boat, and lures a boatload of killers
to destruction on the shoals. The ending is a high-tension
chase that is terminated by a perfectly enormous storm; this
arrives in the nick of time, as storms do in this series.
After this peak of tough excitement, it all oozes away in
goosh:

Guns and crooks seemed very, very far away from the big rambling house, with its apple trees, its lilacs, its old-
fashioned garden, the wall-bordered lane with Blue Gingham
Bay at its foot. A dream world, Calico Lane, through which
one journeyed in eternal peace and security.

Regardless of this drivel, there are a number of hard-
boiled moments during the series. Billy is one of the earliest
figures of the tough crime story. Earlier novelettes combine
wisps of dime novel action with hints of Black Mask ice to
come. In action scenes, the prose grows tightly impelling and
takes on a vaguely hard-boiled tone. Only when the setting is
static does the language change to candy. You can reproduce
the general effect by reading Black Mask while a string quartet
plays sentimental favorites.
A series written, at least in part, by Charles Tyler, that
renowned chronicler of Big Nose Charlie, should shine with
light playfulness. Or so you might expect. But no real laugh-
ter lightens Billy's adventures. The prose stomps soberly
along, intent on the menace, the chase, the bellowing sea storm,
the sentimental tear that stings the eye.
In spite of the narrative style, many stories generate
strong dramatic tension. They climax, if slowly, to endings
that shake with suspense, full of guns and blood. The series
holds your interest, if precariously--and it does so in spite
of all that high-calorie sweetness out Calico Lane way.

THE BLUE JEAN BILLY NOVELETTES

(In *Detective Story Magazine*)

1918
"Raggedy Ann" (March 26)
"Raiders from Raggedy Ann" (July 16)

1919
"Nix's Mate" (March 11)
"The Haunt of Raggedy Ann" (October 7)

1921
"Blue Jean Billy at Fiddler's Reach" (June 25)

1922
"Highway Woman of the Sea" (August 19)

1925
"Blue Jean Billy, Sky Pirate" (April 4)
"Blue Jean Billy and the Lone Survivor" (August 22)

1926
"Blue Jean Billy, Waif of the Sea" (November 6)

1930
"Blue Jean Billy Plays Fair" (January 18)

1931
"Sea Law and Blue Jean Billy" (November 14)

(In *Best Detective*)

"Sky Pirate" (March 1937)
[Reprint of "Blue Jean Billy, Sky Pirate"]

(Continued from page 21)
a single time table for the murder plot, a stronger final clue
--all could have been taken care of in a few hours of writing.
    Even if Carr submitted an unsatisfactory manuscript, it was
the responsibility of the editors at Morrow to check his facts,
bring errors to his attention, and recommend changes. If this
had been done, *The Peacock Feather Murders* would still not be a
great mystery (since the basic idea is unreasonable and there
are other flaws of writing, but it would be a much better book.

Some Thoughts on Peacock Feet

by E.F. Bleiler

I first read *The Peacock Feather Murders* by John Dickson Carr (W.C. Morrow, 1937) quite a few years ago, and I remembered it as a clever, ingenious mystery. Looking back, I now wonder whether my previous estimation of it may not have been colored favorably by the fact that I worked out the solution at the time. On recently rereading it, I found myself disgusted by sloppy gimmicking, loose-end plotting, and careless presentation. After I finished the book, the thought occurred to me that it might be worth while going through it fairly rigorously to see what actually went wrong, and why.

Let me interrupt myself by saying that I am not a fanatic on the matter of "fair play" or pinpoint accuracy. The old-fashioned notion of "fair play" to the reader is a valid way of presenting a story, but there are other ways, too. Nor do I worry greatly about Tonga's lethal darts, or the devil's foot, or the Thin Man's dissolution in quicklime--as long as the story is good and the author does not make a parade of meticulous accuracy. But if an author makes a big to-do about his researches in criminology and the rigors of his gimmicks, it is legitimate to criticize flaws. In *The Peacock Feathers Murders* I think that faking and carelessness run rife.

The story, as is often true of Carr's gimmick books, is based on a single concept, in this instance a particular type of sealed room. A man seems to have been shot twice in a room that was under police observation from both, outside the house and across the hall. The corpse is marked with powder burns, showing that the gun was held close, and the gun itself lies beside the corpse. The carpet is still smouldering from the last discharge. Yet no one (except the victim) had been in the room.

For this discussion I have to reveal Carr's trick and give his explanation of the crime. Actually, the victim was shot once through the window, from the house across the street, and the murder weapon had been tossed through the window into the room. When it landed, it discharged a second time, putting another bullet into the victim and igniting the carpet. One set of powder burns was caused by this discharge. The other set (into which the killer fired) had been inflicted by the murderer in a carefully staged "addident" with a gun loaded with blanks, the day before.

Around this central idea Carr drapes various enveloping elements: the Ten Teacups, a mysterious (fake) secret society that drinks opiated tea and holds orgies; a previous murder that was superficially something like the present murder; and the usual, far-fetched, embarrassing antics of the grotesque, clownish Sir Henry Merrivale.

The locale of the murder is a sealed, watched room. The criminals have tipped off the police, stating the time and place of the crime. The police have a stake-out in the empty house across the street, and they also have a man (Sergeant Pollard) in the murder house itself. Oddly enough, although the police soon know that the crime is scheduled to take place in the attic, they do not venture into the comparable attic room across the way (the houses are all of identical plan), but instead lurk on the ground floor. Perhaps it is just as well, for the murderer walks past them into the attic, does his fell deed, and walks back down. A meeting might have been embarrassing to all.

A similar situation exists on the other side of the street in the murder house. Pollard, although ordered out of the house by the victim, sneaks back in and prowls about, while the victim is blissfully unaware of his presence. Pollard is across the hall from the murder room when death strikes.

Pollard hears two shots, breaks into the room, and finds the corpse of Vance Keating, wealthy playboy, young man about town, lecher, and (it would seem from his actions) monomaniac. The room is fifteen feet by fifteen feet, with one door and a five-and-a-half-by-four-foot window. In the center of the room is a five-foot-round table, upon which are teacups, a couple of which are smashed. Keating's corpse lies extended between the table and the door, parallel to the window. Beside him is a semi-antique revolver, a Remington .45 1894 six-shooter, which has just been fired. Pollard rushes to the window, leans out, and sees nothing unusual. His colleagues across the street inform him that no one has leaped from the window, which is not surprising, since it is about forty feet to the ground.

Within this sequence of events, which shall be analyzed in some detail later, Carr states (as Carr): "A heavy revolver had been fired twice behind that door" (Pocket Book edition, p. 31). This, of course, is a deliberate misstatement, a very unfair misdirection, for, as has already been revealed, the revolver was discharged only once "behind that door."

Let us consider the crime as Carr later states it happened. The murderer, Ron Gardner, a friend of Keating's, has set things up so that at 5:00 p.m. Keating will be standing in the murder room with his back to the window. Gardner then fires at the singed area on the back of Keating's head.

This target is undoubtedly small, perhaps three or four inches across, and the distance of the target is uncertain, since Carr waffles about it. In one place he states that the street is twenty yards wide and talks of areaways and steps. If one adds the street width, areaways, steps, and probable sidewalks, one reaches a window-to-window distance of perhaps seventy to eighty feet. Yet elsewhere Carr states that the window-to-window distance is about sixty feet, comparing it to the distance on a cricket field, sixty-six feet between wickets.

Could Gardner have hit, center on, a target three or four inches across at a range of somewhere between sixty and eighty feet? It is certainly not impossible, but it would be tricky. I am judging here from my own experiences with a Colt .45 in World War II. On an Army firing range, the bull's-eye was

five inches across, and the range was either forty-five feet
or seventy-five feet. Bull's-eyes with such a target and distance were certainly not impossible, but they were difficult
even under optimal conditions: a measured range, good weather,
a familiar weapon, and more than one shot. But when one considers poor lighting (which Carr makes quite a point of, for
reasons which will emerge later), no possibility of making
trial shots to get the range and correct deflection, an unfamiliar, semi-antique weapon of uncertain accuracy, my feeling is that only a fool or a lunatic would risk a halter
around his neck by trying to kill a man with a single shot.
This is not an Oswald situation.

But before Gardner can send his bullet through Keating's
head, he must face the problem of getting the bullet through
the window area, and here he will have tight squeezes and
ticklish passages.

The window is an oblong affair, five and a half feet wide
by four feet high. It is draped with heavy velvet curtains,
which are partly drawn, although the amount of closing is not
indicated--enough, anyway, to darken the room, but not enough
to make sight impossible. The window itself is a sash window;
witnesses saw Keating open it by pushing it up (p. 21).

The dimensions of this window complicate matters considerably and are likely to turn Gardner's shot into a marginal
matter, perhaps possible, equally, perhaps impossible. A window is normally installed two feet from the floor, which would
bring the top of the window six feet from the floor--except
that we do not know exactly what Carr meant by his dimensions.
In millwork descriptions, windows are usually measured by sash
size, and the sashes cut into a certain amount of the glass
area or the aperture area. Keating is described as a middle-
sized man, say 5' 8" tall, 5' 9" tall; this means that the bullet must enter the window at a height 5' 6" to 5' 8" from the
floor. Gardner's target area is thus very close to the edge
of visibility for him.

Let us give Gardner the benefit of doubt in this case and
assume that Keating's burn was not concealed, for we face much
graver problems in the position of the window openings. These
will affect both the shot and the gun-tossing. Carr twice
states that the window was open at the bottom: when Keating
opened it, and when Pollard leaned out over the sill. This
last action suggests that the bottom was wide open. Nowhere
does Carr mention the top window, yet, as will be shown, the
top had to be open, and within certain limits. The point is
not just a quibble on my part, for whether Carr mentioned the
fact or not, the amount of opening is crucial to the crime.

There are three possibilities for the positions of the top
and bottom halves. The top may be closed and the bottom completely open, as is suggested in the story. In this case, the
crime is impossible, for the bullet would have had to smash
through the glass. The second possibility, that the top is
wide open and the bottom closed at the time of the crime seems
ruled out by the story description; it would also, as will be
shown later, render the gun toss impossible. The third possibility, that both top and bottom are open, seems necessary,
but this sets up important space limitations: the minimum the
top could be open (to permit a bullet to pass through at about
5' 6" to 5' 8") is six or seven inches. This limits the bottom
opening (since the individual sashes would be larger than

twenty-four inches, to overlap in the middle) to a maximum of
sixteen inches or so.
Let us return to Gardner and the main gimmick. After making his shot, he throws the gun across the street in such a
manner that it sails through the window, lands on the floor
between the corpse and the window, and obligingly shoots Keating again. The gun must have passed through the bottom aperture, for if it had passed through the top opening (six or
seven inches minimum), at a height of almost six feet, it
would have sailed across the room and probably would have
struck the wall. But passing through the bottom opening
evokes doubts. The gun would have had to enter at a height
of two to three feet, and then its trajectory, within a hori-
zontal component of five or six feet, would have had to descend
to zero. Tricky, tricky. A ballistics expert would have to
determine whether such a path is possible, but I have my doubts.
How about Gardner's throw? Carr states that Gardner was a
first-class cricket bowler, which means that Gardner could
(after much practice) throw a ball weighing about five and a
half ounces some sixty-six feet with precision--though not unfailingly. Could Gardner have thrown a cricket ball seventy
to eighty feet through an opening at most sixteen inches high?
Probably, though not unfailingly.
Could Gardner have thrown an irregularly shaped object like
a gun through this aperture? That is another question.
Carr calls the murder weapon "the original Remington six-
shooter, made in 1894" (p. 34), a description that is not correct. The only .45 six-shooter made in 1894 by the Remington
Company would have been the Model 1890. The previous model,
with which Carr seems to have confused the 1890, was the Im-
proved Frontier Revolver Six Shot, which was still available
in 1888. The 1888 (based on an 1875 model) weighed two pounds,
one ounce, and was fourteen inches long. The 1890 seems to
have been a little lighter and perhaps half an inch shorter.
(Apologies for not being precise here, but the basic book,
Karr's *Remington Handguns*, has been stolen from my local library by some gun collector.)
How would Gardner have thrown a fourteen-inch object
through a space that could at most be sixteen inches? A
cricket player or quoit player throws under hand; a baseball
player throws over hand; a football player pegs; a discus
thrower scales his discus. Does Gardner have much freedom of
choice, since he has a window opening to worry about at his own
end, too? He is not standing free in an open field. How can
he minimize rotation of the flying object, for there is the
horrible possibility that the gun will be an inch or two from
absolute center and strike its long axis against the sashes or
the sill? Scaling is probably the safest technique, but throw-
wing a cricket ball is hardly likely to make one an expert
scaler.
Getting the gun into the room is difficult enough, and
edges into impossibility, but Carr is unwilling to let matters
stand at this extreme degree of improbability. He advances
into more complications. "There was Keating's body stretched
out like a target with its back to him just beyond a window
five and a half feet wide.... With luck he could put another
bullet into Keating" (p. 228).
Now here we fall into complete impossibility. Gardner
could not have seen Keating's body nor known where it fell.

There is no need to invoke the poor visibility outside, nor
limitations of vision caused by partially closed drapes; the
situation is a simple problem in geometry. Since the houses
are identical and the windows are at the same height, a right
triangle is formed. The base is six feet, Gardner's eye
height. (I shall use round figures to make calculation easier.) The second side of the triangle is created by the floors
of the two houses, extended on. The hypotenuse of the triangle
is Gardner's line of vision, striking at the window sill of the
house opposite, some seventy feet away. As can be easily cal-
culated, Gardner's line of vision will pass well over the
corpse, which is about five or six feet from the window. The
corpse will not become completely visible until it is 105 feet
away!

The position of the corpse is also odd. When Pollard en-
tered the room, he found Keating lying "at full length on the
floor between the table and the door, head toward the door. He
was lying on his left side." The revolver "lay on the floor at
his left side," by which I assume Carr means that the revolver
was at Keating's back. But this positioning does not fit either
the properties of the room or Carr's later description of how
the corpse fell. The space between the table and door must be
five feet, within which a 5' 8" or so corpse is to be extended
at full length. Even if we assume that Carr was expressing
himself loosely, and meant that Keating's legs were well under
the table, it is very difficult to see how Keating could have
arrived at his final position. "I see Keating standin' with
his back to the window.... He pitched across the table, smashing two teacups on a slightly different side of the clock-dial.
He pulls the tablecloth a bit, rolls off, and lands on his
left-hand side" (p. 227). But this brings the head of the
corpse several feet away from the position in which Pollard
found it, with the body at a different angle.

To summarize our ingenious crime: We have a murderer who
ignores the presence of the police, who generously reciprocate
by ignoring him, and places a single shot with unerring accuracy, at long range for a pistol, under very poor lighting conditions, with an unfamiliar weapon, into a target that he may
not be able to see. The position of the window sashes across
the street must be optimal, or else broken glass will destroy
the illusion of place. He then flings a fairly heavy, strangely
shaped object--without previous practice--through a small space
about seventy feet away, even though the large dimensions of
the object are almost certain to spoil his throw. This object
assumes a peculiarly convenient trajectory and lands beside a
totally invisible corpse that the murderer is under the delu-
sion that he can see. I won't animadvert on the likelihood of
the second shot's striking the corpse, since Carr places this
within the purlieus of chance and that is his right.

The police, who were looking up, saw nothing of this. They
did not see a fourteen-inch gun sailing sixty to eighty feet,
clearing the sill, and entering the room. Why not? Carr says,
first, that the day was very dark and the sky overcast, with a
storm brewing. Birdwatchers will not be convinced by this
argument. Second, that the window through which the cops were
watching was so dirty that they couldn't see anything. Carr
makes a footnoted reference to the fact that Pollard, when he
arrived at the scene and looked in the window, could see nothing.
This is, of course, a red herring, for visibility through dirty

windows is usually one-sided, and Carr destroys his own case
by permitting the policeman on the other side of the dirty
window to recognize Pollard with no difficulty whatever.

Obviously, there are many things wrong with this conjec-
tural crime, even for a work of fiction, yet, surprisingly
enough, many of them could have been avoided or palliated by
a few simple changes that Carr should have thought of or that
his editors should have suggested. Why didn't someone think
of using a slightly higher *casement* window and setting the
crime at night?

This is the first murder within the action of the story.
(I shall not comment on a previous teacup murder that is only
talked about and is indirectly connected to the story-present.
But it, too, has difficulties.) Toward the end of the book a
second murder occurs. The-man-who-knew-too-much (Keating's
valet, Bartlett) is knifed in a remarkable coincidence of
split-second timing.

Gardner, the murderer, has been tailed around town by a
detective whom Masters has assigned as a routine matter. Gardner has spotted the tail and has led him on a long chase which
ends at the house that has been announced for a third murder in
the Ten Teacups series. (In this case the announcement was
simply a blind to provide a circumstance for an unravelment.)
Gardner, who was a few feet ahead of his tail, came along at
the precise moment when Bartlett was opening the door to the
house, and he threw a knife into the valet's back. Bartlett
staggered into the house and died. The police--who had the
house staked out--and the tail saw nothing of this.

Now for the disposition of Bartlett's corpse--and here I
must admit some admiration is mingled with dissatisfaction.
Soar, one of the secondary suspects, seems to be trapped in the
house with a highly suspicious corpse. But, with the police
thumping at the door, he is equal to the situation. He picks
up the corpse, places it in a wicker chair, props it up with
boards, puts a board on its lap, ties its limbs in place so
that it cannot flop, slams a dust cover over it, and then sits
on the corpse pretending that it is a chair. Only H.M. notices
that the chair looks odd.

As Dr. Johnson said of, I believe, Parson Dodd, the knowledge that one is going to die quickens one's faculties enor-
mously. This comment is especially appropriate, since Soar
states (and the time table supports him), "I did it in not much
more than two minutes."

†

This book deserves a C-minus in mechanisms, but perhaps
motivations and solution will be stronger.

The murder situation revolves around three personalities:
Keating, the victim; Gardner, the killer; and Mrs. Derwent, a
femme fatale. To consider Mrs. Derwent first, since she is
central. She is a junoesque mass of voluptuousness who is married to a slightly senescent man decades her senior. Her specialty is mankilling. She is a tease of the worst sort, but
really nearly frigid. Her husband, who is sick of her, would
be delighted to catch her in adultery and divorce her, but she
only entices and never satisfies. (It is revealed at the end,
however, that she is having an affair with Gardner, who is
madly in love with her.)

This siren has captivated Keating, who has sworn to his friends that he will not stop pursuing her until he "has made that bitch come across." Thus, when he learns of the society of the Ten Teacups, with the peacock feathers, opium, and orgies, he is eager to join, since he has also been told that Mrs. Derwent is a member and thereby will have to "come across" to him at the next orgy.

Keating is not motivated solely by lust. He is a nasty fellow, and he wants revenge for having been teased. He makes a plan, for which he is willing to undergo much inconvenience and expense. First, he makes a will in favor of Mrs. Derwent and lets it be known to her. This is counterenticement. The will is usually dated June 28th, although Mr. Derwent, a solicitor, who had no reason to lie or be deceived, places it late in July. But then Derwent is himself a numerical problem. On page seventy-four, Carr, as author, states that "he might have been a few years past sixty," but by page 185 Derwent has aged to over seventy.

Secretly, unknown to even his closest friends, after making the will Keating has married Miss Gale, the ingenue of the novel, with the (successful) intention of secretly invalidating the will to Mrs. Derwent. Keating cares nothing about Miss Gale, whose reasons for marrying him are obscure, since she really loves Gardner. In addition to a wife acquired for the purpose of upsetting his own will, Keating also buys, at a moment's notice, the murder house for £3,500. This is to ensure a proper meeting place for the (mythical) society of Ten Teacups. This purchase is simply an oral agreement, which Carr then indicates amounts to transfer of ownership. I do not know how this stands in British law, and I cannot contradict it, despite my suspicions that it is not correct. But I do know that in American common law, in most (or all, perhaps?) states, an oral agreement is definitely not considered binding for real estate transfer.

Keating's purpose behind these shenanigans is setting up a situation. As he gloatingly projects it to himself, after he has laid Mrs. Derwent in the teacup orgy she will roll over and murmur, "Darling, that was wonderful. I'll get a divorce and we can get married right away." Whereupon he will say, "Sorry, Baby. No dice. I'm already married. Ha, ha, ha." (Conversation mine, not Carr's.)

Mrs. Derwent and Gardner, however, have their own plans for Keating. They plan to murder him. But why and since when are questionable, for Carr generously offers two time tables. First, Mrs. Derwent and Gardner started their plan after Keating made his will. H.M. says, "Janet Derwent murdered calmly for money" (p. 232), and H.M. states that Mrs. Derwent planned her murder alibi two weeks ahead. In this scheme, Gardner goes along for love of Mrs. Derwent. But if all this seems too brief, one can take the longer time table. Here Gardner set up the Ten Teacups hoax perhaps a year to a year and a half before the murder. Gardner, who is one of Carr's sleazy sportsman-cum-explorer he-man types, has written a book about his travels in Brazil, and in the book he describes a (mythical) branch of the Ten Teacups flourishing in the jungles. This book must have been in print for some time before the murder, for Miss Gale considers it reasonable that the detectives might have read it.

As Carr well knew, publishing a book from MS to finished

product usually takes a year or so. To this must be added time for circulation. The beginning of the plot is now far back in the past, before there was any reason for the crime: Keating's will. "You don't mean he deliberately shoved a lie into a book that was supposed to be true, so that later, when it seemed to come true in London, there'd be confirmation?" "Why not?..." "That shows a long degree of premeditation" (pp. 230-231).

But let us abandon origins, a year and a half ago, June 28th, around July 25th, or so, and consider the clue that broke the case for H.M.

H.M. first sees light by questioning the testimony of Keating's valet, Bartlett. The valet made several statements of importance: that the wad from the blank cartridge that caused the powder burn struck a glass in a tray that he was holding and caused him to drop the tray; that Keating was holding the gun with the blanks when it went off (untrue; it was Gardner, as part of the plot; Bartlett lied on Keating's instructions); that Gardner had been in Keating's apartment with Bartlett until a short time before the murder of Keating (true).

This last point, Keating's alibi, involved Carr in a timetable dilemma which he did not try to surmount, but, instead, bluffed. Carr very candidly states that Gardner might have reached the place of the murder at the announced time, 5:00 p.m., if he had had perfect transportation connections. But he leaves the reader wondering why Gardner, whose plan called for precision in time and place, did not leave early enough to be sure that he would be at the murder spot at 5:00 p.m. But here is the dilemma: if Gardner had left earlier, he would have had no half alibi from Bartlett, and Carr would have had to think up something else.

To return to H.M.'s clue. He questions Bartlett's statement that the wad only broke a glass, and asserts that the explosion would have almost incinerated Bartlett. He goes into a long tirade about blank cartridges which have caused serious burns on persons many feet away, etc., until the reader wonders whether Carr has not confused a blank cartridge with a flame thrower. One also wonders, if H.M.'s gruesome anecdotes are to be taken seriously, why Keating was not much more seriously injured.

There are probably blank cartridges and blank cartridges, I'll admit, but I have fired a fair number, and I have never seen effects like those H.M. describes. But even if H.M.'s theory of burning is accepted, Carr ignores the possibility that Bartlett may have been telling the truth: the wad simply ricocheted from Keating's head.

After H.M.'s rather dubious insight, the unraveling takes its expected course. At the moment when the murderer is about to be named, he steps into the room with a grand gesture. H.M. explains all the oddities--not convincingly. Mrs. Derwent will presumably go free and continue her raids on masculinity, though perhaps as a divorced woman. The mystery is over; the fake secret society exploded; and the noose is prepared for Gardner.

†

The sad thing about *The Peacock Feather Murders* is that so many of its flaws could have been corrected easily with a few small changes on Carr's part. A casement window, a night crime, one wound in the corpse, credible dimensions and measurements,
(Continued on page 13)

It's About Crime

By Marvin Lachman

If you, too, are a graduate of Ebenezer Scrooge U., I have the perfect antidote to the annual era of good feeling. It's Avon's *Twelve Crimes of Christmas* ($2.50), edited by Isaac Asimov, Martin H. Greenberg, and Carol-Lynn Rössel Waugh. Asimov, in an introduction, succinctly describes the origins of the holiday. It's a good anthology with such highlights as Queen's "The Dauphin's Doll," Stout's "Christmas Party," Ellin's "Death on Christmas Eve," John Dickson Carr's "Blind Man's Hood," Hoch's "The Problem of the Christmas Steeple," and a little-known, delightfully off-beat story, "Do your Christmas Shoplifting Early," by Robert Somerlott.

What are the odds on two mysteries called *Who's On First* coming out in the same year? It happened in 1979. One was by William F. Buckley. The other, by Joan Allan, was one of Zebra's books ($1.95) with the misleading illustrated clues, unbelievable dialogue, and shameless brand-name dropping. Marketed expressly for a female audience, they all have "new-breed" women as detectives. Among the occupations of Zebra series detectives are professor, artist, ballet dancer, actress, country and western singer, photographer, reporter, gossip columnist, and nurse. Only Norma Schier's books are decently written; she also has a believable sleuth, Kay Barth, an assistant district attorney who might be expected to get involved in murder. Allan's book is definitely not recommended.

Morris Hershman has written few books under his own name, but he has done a slew of Gothics as Evelyn Bond. He's back, writing as Sam Victor, with a series for Charter regarding Talbot Lion, the President's half-brother, trouble-shooter, and "one of the world's best known studs." In *White House Massacre* ($2.25) Lion takes time out from a *ménange à trois* with two swinging women to solve the disappearance of a nuclear "pencil" bomb. In *Cuban Inferno* ($2.25) Lion is involved when the President is wounded on his way to denounce Castro at the U.N. (It's a half-assassination book.)

While reading Herbert Adams' *The Golden Ape* (1930), I had the feeling I was the only person in the United States reading Adams at that moment; I probably was. Adams has done some good things in the past, but this is not one of them. In fact, he sets a world's record in withholding clues from the reader. He is still a readable author, even if he does drag in irrelevant conversations about his great love, golf. He also has a Scotland Yard inspector who says, "If everyone was in bed by twelve, you could close half the prisons."

In *Photo Finish* (Jove, $2.50), Ngaio Marsh tells an old-fashioned (yet modern) tale of murder on an island isolated by a storm. She even brings Roderick and Troy Alleyn back to her beloved New Zealand. It's an enjoyable, civilized book about a Maria Callas-type opera singer, but muddled detection and an unbelievable use of the Mafia in the plot prevent it from being as good as it should have been. Jove has also reprinted an earlier Marsh, *The Nursing Home Murder* ($2.50), which she wrote with the assistance of Dr. Henry Jellett, using background she obtained while hospitalized for over three months. It's one of her best and is surprisingly undated (it was first published in 1935), despite its background of British politics and medicine. Incidentally, in England a nursing home is a hospital, not a residence facility for the infirm elderly.

Max Byrd's *California Thriller* (Bantam, $2.25) is one of those recent books with dumb titles (another is Gene Thompson's *Murder Mystery*). Byrd's paperback original launches a promising series about a San Francisco private eye, Mike Haller. There is very little reason why detectives should still tell their stories in the first person. What was a novelty when Philip Marlowe did it is now a cliché and leads to awkward use of metaphors. Example: Haller, on awakening from being drugged, says, "A loud bump jolted me awake, and my head floated off. Heat. Unending heat that pressed down like a weight from every direction, a tight thick coffin of heat." First person narration leads to other excesses, e.g., unnecessary wisecracks. Byrd's success rate is only fair. Why is this a promising first novel, then? Because Byrd has a raw vitality to his writing that grabs the reader. He is a good observer of the San Francisco scene, and he almost makes you forget a silly plot by his tremendously suspenseful ending.

Mysteries are everywhere, even in good humor writing, e.g. Woody Allen's *Side Effects* (Ballantine, $2.75), which includes a fine parody of an Existentialist detective story, "The Condemned." Throughout this story (and the book) are examples of Allen's crazy logic, such as "Cloquet protested his innocence, but he was informed that his fingerprints had been found all over Brisseau's room and on the recovered pistol. When he broke into Brisseau's house, Cloquet had also made the mistake of signing the guest book."

Some of the columns collected in Russell Baker's *So This Is Depravity* (Washington Square Press/Pocket Books, 325 pp., $3.50) are related to crime writing, primarily "The Unipedal Mystery," "Gangland Style," and "A Gloom Full of Spies." The last named is a fine parody on the books of Le Carré and Deighton. There are 120 more columns, many of them hilarious, in a book that gives full measure for its money.

A well-known Sherlockian scholar, Trevor H. Hall, has turned to another author with *Dorothy L. Sayers: Nine Literary Studies* (Archon Books, 905 Sherman Ave., Hamden, CT 06514, $19.50). He imparts a great deal of interesting information, including facts about her marriage and the careers of her husband, Atherton Fleming; recollections of Sayers by those who knew her; information about the chronology of the novel/play *Busman's Honeymoon*; and Sayers' attitude toward spiritualism. Almost worth the considerable price alone is an outstanding bit

of literary detective work on the part of Hall as he uncovers
the facts about Robert Eustace, who collaborated with Sayers
on *The Documents in the Case*.
     You won't read a funnier book during 1982 than Jon L.
Breen's *Hair of the Sleuthhound* (Scarecrow Press, 52 Liberty
St., P.O. Box 656, Metuchen, NJ 00840, $12.50). Only someone
who knows and loves mysteries could produce a collection of
stories which so hilariously and accurately parody those on
which they are based. I'll admit to a special fondness for
this form of fiction, but I've read many that were lead bal-
loons. Breen is simply the best writer of parodies around,
and there isn't a bad one in this volume. Only the Jimmy Chin
(Charlie Chan) story is disappointing; Breen once did a much
better pastiche which used Chan's name--"The Fortune Cookie"
(EQMM, May 1971).
     At his best, Breen captures the essence and style of his
subject ("target" is not the operative word, because Breen does
not have to destroy anyone to be humorous). He replicates Ed
McBain's metaphors which, as the 87th Precinct series has pro-
gressed, have become parodies of themselves. His John Dickson
Carr begins, as many of that master's did, with a young couple
meeting "cute" on a train. It is a locked-room story and includes the old footprints-in-the-snow bit. In "The Lithuanian
Eraser Mystery," E. Larry Cune solves, appropriately enough, a
dying-message murder. My favorite story is "The Dog in the
Merger," which gave me more pleasure than any other piece of
short mystery fiction I read in 1973, the year it was first
published. In kidding Emma Lathen, it captures that team's
New York and Wall Street metaphors.
     Sports mysteries are one of Breen's loves, and some of his
parodies are part of that sub-sub-genre. There is a Dick
Francis—type story, "Breakneck," cricket in a Raffles parody,
and "Frank Meriswell's Greatest Case," which is not only de-
lightful but is also the best mystery about basketball I've
read.
     In addition to the authors mentioned above, Breen, in this
bonanza of a book, has fun with Hammett, John D. MacDonald,
J.J. Marric, S.S. Van Dine, Hugh Pentecost, Agatha Christie,
Arthur B. Reeve, Isaac Asimov, Ross Macdonald, Ed Hoch, Mike
Avallone, and Donald Hamilton.
     Nineteen-eighty-one will go down as the year in which
paperback art was recognized. There was Art Scott's presentation at Bouchercon and the books by O'Brien and Schreuders
which I previously reviewed. Everest House capped the year off
by publishing *Agatha Christie: The Art of Her Crimes. The
Paintings of Tom Adams* in hardcover at $24.95. Adams is a
well-known artist who illustrated dozens of Christie's covers
here and in England in the 1960's and 1970's. The original
paintings used for these covers are collectors' items.
     There is an introduction by Jown Fowles (he wrote *The
Collector*) and commentary by Julian Symons to go with ninety of
Adams' paintings. Everest implies that this is a virtually
complete collection of his Christie covers, but I noticed that
the covers for the Pocket Book editions of *Passenger to Frank-
furt* and *Nemesis* (both outstanding works of art) are not in-
cluded. Still, what is here is a treat to the eye, especially
if your taste in art runs toward horror and the surrealistic.
The book contains a dozen or more paintings I wouldn't mind
framing and hanging in my house.

Television and movies may be the impetus, but the publishers are keeping the old masters in print. I suspect that the long-running TV series was responsible for the constant reprinting of Perry Mason books during the years 1957-1970. Recently, Erle Stanley Gardner's long-time publisher, Pocket Books, has forsaken its erstwhile meal ticket, but Ballantine has come along to take up some of the slack. Most recently, they have reprinted The Cases of *The Vagabond Virgin* (1948) and *The Grinning Gorilla* (1952) at $2.25 each. These are two of his best and fastest moving books, with *Gorilla* especially interesting since it is probably the most "exotic" of the entire Mason series.

Bantam is no stranger to Rex Stout's Nero Wolfe, and they are apparently not allowing the failure of last winter's TV series deter them. They have recently published four Stout books to which Pyramid had the rights, and they are all very much worth keeping alive. *The Rubber Band* is my choice for the best of all the Wolfe books. In addition to the great Nero-Archie byplay, it has far and away the most interesting and involved plot structure Stout ever created. It sells at $2.25; at $2.50 Bantam has published *The Red Box* (1937) and *Black Orchids* (1942), the latter containing the famous title novelet and "Cordially Invited to Meet Death," which is even better. Finally, also at $2.50, we get Stout's *The Broken Vase* (1941), one of his brief series about Tecumseh Fox, another detective with an animal's name. This is the book that's notable for a murder at Carnegie Hall and an exciting car race against time from Manhattan to Brewster, New York. If only Stout had spent as much time and care on his plots after World War II as he did in his early books, a very good series would have been "most satisfactory."

With theatre and television movies abounding, Pocket Books keeps reprinting Agatha Christie. On behalf of each new generation of readers, I bless them. *Easy to Kill* (1939, $2.50) is one of her non-series books, though a pivotal character, Miss Fullerton, resembles Miss Marple and is described as a "wooly-minded old lamb." She has that inate suspicion that so many Christie spinsters possess. Believing that it is easy to disguise murders as accidents, she brings three such occurrences to the attention of retired policeman Luke Fitzwilliam and begins an investigation herself.

Murder Is Easy was on television last year; *Evil Under the Sun* (1941, $2.75) is apparently an enormous success, at prices much greater than the book, in first-run movie theatres. Universal Pictures has jazzed up Christie's original story with an international cast, a screenplay by Anthony Shaffer, and a change of locale from a resort in Southern England to the supposedly more glamorous Adriatic. What I hope they haven't spoiled is a gem of a plot, one in which Christie fooled me, as she was to do so many times.

DEATH OF A MYSTERY WRITER

Edward Corley died in November 1981 in Mississippi at the age of fifty. He wrote *Genesis Rock, Air Force One,* and *Hijacked* under his own name. The last was filmed as *Skyjacked* with Charleston Heston. Corley also wrote as William Judson, David Harper, and (with Jack Murphy) as Patrick Buchanan.

Dorothy Eden died on March 4, 1982, at age 69 in London. She wrote about thirty books, mostly in the Gothic suspense field, with another book due in May.

Philip K. Dick died on March 2, 1982, at age 54 in Santa Ana, California. Better known for his science fiction, he combined that genre with mystery in *A Maze of Death* (1970) and *Flow My Tears, the Policeman Said* (1974).

Ayn Rand died in New York on March 6, 1982, at age 77. Better known for her novels and Objectivist philosophy, she also, early in her career, wrote a mystery play, *The Night of January 16th* (1935), in which the audience is asked to judge the verdict of a murder trial on stage.

Marietta S. Shaginyan died at the age of 93 in the USSR. According to her obit in the *New York Times*, "In the early years of literary ferment after the revolution she experimented with a variety of styles and pioneered in developing the Soviet detective novel, combining a mystery plot with revolutionary ideology." Two of her books in this genre, *Laurie Lane, the Metalworker* and *Mess Mend, or the Yankees in Petrograd*, were written under the pen name "Jimmy Dollar," supposedly an American worker in Russia.

Dame Ngaio Marsh died in Christchurch, New Zealand, at the age of 82.

(Continued from page 4)
    The tour begins at the north-west corner of 50th Street and Sixth Avenue (Avenue of the Americas) at 2:00 p.m. on Saturday, June 26, 1982, and is open to the public. In case of rain, the tour will be held on Sunday, June 27th.
    For further information, please contact The Maltese Falcon Society, c/o Judith Freeman, One Bogardus Place, New York, NY 10040.

    And finally, for the Sherlockians in our midst, Paulette Green advises that she will be publishing, this fall, Madeleine B. Stern's monograph *The Game's a Head: A Phrenological Study of Sherlock Holmes, with a Phrenological Case Study of Sir Arthur Conan Doyle.* More details in the next TMF.

(Continued from page 5)
Death at Lord's (Gollancz, 1952).
The Wishful Think (Hale, 1954).
Double Menace (Hale, 1954).
Operation Barbarossa (Hale, 1956).
The Otan Plot (Hale, 1957).
The Silver Greyhound (Hale, 1960).
This Is Your Life (Hale, 1963).
The Traveling Executioners (Hale, 1964).
The Spy at No. 10 (Hale, 1965).
Evil Phoenix (Hale, 1966).
Draw the Dragon's Teeth (Hale, 1967).
The Jail-Breakers (Hale, 1968).

Reel Murders

Movie Reviews by Walter Albert

Silent Rage (1982). Director: Michael Miller.

Silent Rage is the annual Chuck Norris action melodrama, an event that seems to attract the kind of involved, excitable audience the early Clint Eastwood films drew into the theaters. I saw this on a Sunday night with my seventeen-year-old son in a suburban theater with an audience of young wiseacres, some motorcycle freaks, and a smattering of older couples who looked as if they would have been more comfortable watching the American Film Institute tribute to good-hearted Frank Capra.

Local reviewers--who apparently loved the film even while hating it--have criticized Norris for his blatant use of the psychotic horrors of the Halloween-type film and have missed the point that this is not just Halloween Whatever but Frankenstein 1982. I must admit that it is good to welcome back the devoted, amoral scientist who gives life to a powerful, inhuman creature and cries out in the best Colin Clive tradition, "We're scientists, not moralists!" This time there are three devoted scientists: a good, moral type with a beard and a lovely, talented wife; an intermediate scientist who knows that what he's doing is wrong but continues to do it with a perpetually perplexed knotting of his forehead; and the super-baddy who has a neat moustache and burning eyes and keeps repairing the monster when it returns to the laboratory after each of its murderous sorties.

Settings are always handsome in Chuck Norris films. The laboratory is bathed in a penumbral, soft green light that kept distracting me from the actors when they babbled on too long about their great work and its unfortunate consequences. The art director also designed an attractive house for the good doctor and his artistic wife, with stairs into the basement and up to the attic so that the monster can chase people up and down a lot. Norris has moved from his expensive town house on the bay in last year's *Eye for an Eye* into a frame structure with a multi-level living room nestled among the pines and a deck that looks out onto a cycloramic shot of mountains. (I just wish that movie-makers would master the art of meshing these rear-screen projections with the actors' foreground posturings.) The monster spends most of his time lurching about the good doctor's house or lying on his table and peering slyly at the unobservant doctors who think he's unconscious. The green lab is his home and some jaundiced types may wonder why

monsters have to have more attractive surroundings than ordinary
folk. The bad doctor has an apartment in the hospital, but it's
a functional, undistinguished place that suggests he's insensitive to his living space--if not to his working space--and probably makes an implicit statement about his limited moral sense.
The middle-sized bear--sorry--the middle doctor doesn't seem to
live anywhere but the laboratory and will probably remind some
of you of professors you had in college who looked like fish
out of water when you met them walking on campus.
    The dilemma in the film is the problem Norris--a fancy judo
type--has in dealing with a creature who just wants to break
his neck or spine or slam him up against a wall. The creature
also has a limited ability to repair itself, is almost inde-
structible, and couldn't care less for the niceties of the
carefully choreographed Norris style. Coincidence solves that
problem and it may or not satisfy you.
    The most spectacular scene is the obligatory one in which a
character is flung through a closed window and the camera catches
him in mid-air amidst showering slivers of glass. The director
and cameraman are very professional, and, while I may have
treated this film with a light touch, it's probably because I
was a nervous wreck by the end of it, and the various chases and
fights are real nerve tinglers.
    Norris is his usual likeable, unflappable self. In his
first appearance in the film, he walks up on the porch and
knocks on the screen door of a house in which a clearly certi-
fiable loony has just axed two people. To me, this captures
the essence of the Norris persona, with a polite respect for
rules but the willingness to deploy great physical skill to
combat the baddies when it is clear that violence is the only
solution.
    Whatever else may be happening on the screen and in the
real world these days, it's good to know that the mad scientist
and his fiendish creation are still running amok on neighbor-
hood screens and that right still triumphs over might. But
don't despair--the final frame of the film is right out of
Halloween and all its imitators and don't be surprised next
summer to find me reporting on *Silent Rage II.*

SHORT TAKES

Evil Under the Sun (1982). Director: Guy Hamilton.

    In a recent issue of the *Times Literary Supplement,* Julian
Symons complained mightily about the betrayal of the Christie
novel on which this is based. Chris Steinbrunner, in the July
1982 EQMM, recognized the tinkering with the novel but thought
the result was splendid. I haven't read the novel, but, apart
from competent performances by good actors--of whom the most
amusing are Peter Ustinov, Maggie Smith, and Diana Rigg (whose
archness is, however, beginning to wear thin)--good tunes by
Cole Porter attractively orchestrated by John Lanchbery, and
handsome location filming on Majorca, there is no reason to pay
more than a bargain matinee admission for this film. It is too
long, the narrative sags intermittently as the camera doodles
across the landscape and sets, and there is the curse of a
campy performance by Roddy MacDowell as a critic who is probably
modelled on the insufferable Rex Reed. This might warm you if

there's a blinding snowstorm outside, but this is television
fare dressed up as a big screen offering.

Bluebeard (1944). Director: Edgar G. Ulmer.

John Carradine plays a disturbed puppeteer dubbed "Bluebeard" by the Parisian tabloids in this stylish, low-budget
film. In the twenties Ulmer worked as a production designer
on films directed by F.W. Murnau and Fritz Lang, and the
theatrical-looking studio sets (including what appears to be
a cardboard cutout of Notre Dame) are appropriate to this study
of a deranged artist. The most striking visual effect is a
shot of the puppeteer's eye peering out balefully at the
audience in the park--and, coincidentally, at the theater
audience. It reminds me of a shot in Lang's *You Only Live
Once* (1937) in which the blind covering the rear window of a
menacing black automobile parts to reveal a pair of eyes, the
face covered as if by a mask in an imaginative use of the melo-
dramatic convention of the hooded villain. Carradine plays the
role of the artist/murderer with great restraint, and his long
face and mournful eyes, wedded to his rich but monochromatic
voice, give to his performance the haunting--or haunted--look
of a fallen angel.

Peeping Tom (1959). Director: Michael Powell.

Tom is a young photographer (English, but played incon-
gruously by German actor Carl Boehm) who photographs the death-
scenes of young women who imagine that he is giving them screen-
tests. Boehm's flat performance is chilling, and I find this
film as disquiting as Hitchcock's *Psycho*. The camera eye
seduces the victims and the audience, and there is an extended,
bravura sequence in a film studio that portrays the protagonist's heightened sexual excitement so graphically that many
viewers may find it intensely disturbing. The film was a box-
office failure when it was first released (at a time when
audiences preferred the Hammer films' tamer eroticism) and
virtually put an end to Powell's film career. The director of
such distinguished films as *Black Narcissus, The Red Shoes,* and
The Tales of Hoffman photographs this in bright, glossy color
that make the scenes of violence all the more disturbing. You
may find this film disgusting, but I don't think you will be
insensitive to its power.

(Continued from page 43)
Robin Winks recently confessed that this series is better
than he had thought it was, which only goes to show that Yale
history professors can have second thoughts and subscribe to
the revisionist school of reviewing. Or, as Ellen Nehr might
put it, if Winks likes it, it can't be that good. No real attempt at characterization, Marshall specializing in the anec-
dote rather than the novel, but the final fireworks are spec-
tacular--in the predictable Marshall fashion--and since the
author leaps quickly from one scene to another, the jokes go
by so quickly that even if they're bad--as they often are--they
are casual enough to be acceptable. (Walter Albert)

Mystery*File

Short Reviews by Steve Lewis

Steve Allen. *The Talk Show Murders*. Delacorte Press, 1982, 314 pp., $12.95.

It so happens that I think Steve Allen is an unrecognized genius. If you take a look at the ratings of his last few television ventures, I think you'll agree on at least half of that statement.

The fact remains that this is his twenty-fourth book, and some of them are a sight more serious than *Bop Fables*, which was his first. There was *Ripoff: A Look at Corruption in America*, for example, a factual exposé of white collar crime in this country--not exactly what you'd expect to see as number one on the laugh parade.

This is his first mystery novel. Being a celebrity of some renown, Steve Allen should expect to sell a few more copies of this book than would the author of your average whodunit detective story. I'm happy for Mr. Allen, but I'm caught in a quandry of mixed emotions, since the book is only marginally better than that same average whodunit detective story mentioned above.

Naturally, the subject matter is an ideal one. The first death occurs on Toni Tennille's show, the second on Johnny Carson. Phil Donahue is next, followed by Dick Cavett, then a grand finale of a showdown on The Merv Griffen Show. Steve Allen no longer has a show to call his own--what a shame!--but he knows his way around backstage--and frontstage--and his capsule descriptions of the other hosts no longer his competition are the other reason you'll read this book.

The first, of course, is the mystery. The sequence of killings quickly becomes a personal challenge aimed directly at Roger Dale, the private eye working on the case. Roger Dale is a P.I. with an eye for PR--public relations, that is. All of the victims are advance-guard members of the sexual revolution presumed to be sweeping the country, another clue for Dale to add to his PP of the killer--the psychological profile.

In the end, just as they always used to do, all of the suspects are gathered together in one room--in this case, the nation's living room!--live and direct, as they always say, to find out who the guilty one is. It is the talk show to end all talk shows--and if it hadn't worked, it probably would have.

As a detective-story writer, Allen does not play fair in the classical sense. Even Roger Dale himself is not sure whom he'll name as the killer before he finally wrings a confession

out of him/her while still on the air. There are no real clues
for the reader to eagerly snap up along the way.

It's still nothing less than a huge amount of gripping fun
to read, which in this case has to be the single, number-one
criterion. (B)* (*Reviews so marked have appeared earlier in
the Hartford *Courant*.)

Leslie Ford. *The Clue of the Judas Tree*. Dell, 1933, 240 pp.

In several ways it's hard to believe this book was written
almost fifty years ago. The writing is remarkably fresh and
relevant, even if the characters and the setting are out of the
pages of history, if not history books, per se.

For example, the Crash of Wall Street in 1929 is still very
much on everyone's mind when it comes to matters financial, and
the person who is the immediate suspect when financier Duncan
Trent is found murdered is a shell-shock victim of World War I.

"Psychology" is an important ingredient in this early cross
between a gothicky novel overwhelming apprehension and a
strictly-playing-it-by-the-clues detective story, and so is
romance.

The ending is unusually cluttered, but then perhaps it had
to be to explain away all that had happened. Dashiell Hammett,
one suspects, would not have had patience with a story like
this, nor with the sort of fantasy world it takes place in, but
it's a branch of the detective novel that certainly seemed to
blossom about the same time as *The Maltese Falcon*. This book
is not still in print, but it could be--and its descendants,
either direct or indirect, certainly are! (B minus)

Charlotte MacLeod. *Wrack and Rune*. Doubleday/Crime Club,
1982, 180 pp., $10.95.

Charlotte MacLeod is a relative newcomer to the field of
mystery writing, but in the past two or three years she has
certainly shown all the signs of becoming a name to reckon
with.

Agatha Christie is no longer with us, but even if she were,
she'd have no cause for fear. What makes these adventures of
Peter Shandy so highly anticipated, at least in some circles,
is hardly the detection involved, though there is that, too.
Instead, it's the pure laugh-out-loud sort of humor that per-
vades MacLeod's stories; that, plus the fact that the large
proportion of her characters, many of them old friends to us
now, actually *like* each other.

Shandy is a professor of agrology at Balaclava College, up
somewhere in nearby Massachusetts, but his fame at becoming
involved in cases of murder has spread from the campus clear
across Balaclava County, clearly the wildest piece of country
this side of Appalachia.

A runestone found in an ancient farmstead may be the har-
binger of buried Viking treasure to come. The prospect brings
out the worst in some people, and before you can say Thorkjeld
Svenson more than the college experts have quickly overrun the
site.

Death by quicklime also results, as well as a few other
assorted attempts at murder. There's never been such excite-

ment in Lumpkin Corners as this ever before.
This particular outing, Shandy's third appearance now, may
be too long by about a third for a constant level of such inspired insanity to be properly maintained, but I doubt you'll
have as much fun with a detective novel as you will with this
one.
That is, until the next one. (C plus)*

Peter Rabe, *My Lovely Executioner*. Gold Medal, 1960, 143 pp.

It's my opinion--and so far's I know, nobody else's--that
Peter Rabe should have a name in the mystery field comparable
to some of those writing in the heyday of *Black Mask*. No, not
a top-notcher like Hammett or Chandler, but more along the
lines of a Raoul Whitfield, say.
Like the one at hand, much of Rabe's work seems to have
been devoted to inside glimpses into life in the underworld.
Tough, sexy, hard-boiled--all are adjectives that seem to apply.
To a certain extent, it occasionally takes some work to read
in between the lines Rabe wrote, as if you really had to think
like a crook to make the pieces of the puzzle fit together the
way they should.
This one opens with a guy named Gallivan as he's being
busted out of prison. Non-voluntarily, it should be added.
He has only three weeks to go before his time is up. Now he's
on the run, aided by the prison-mate who helped spring him and
a girl named Jessie whom the other guy seems to know.
Gallivan's problem is threefold: what's their motive; how
can he escape them; and *should* he escape them? Add another:
can he escape them?
Not a major story, by any means. There are no big scenes
that stand out in your memory afterwards, ones you'd auto-
matically think of when you think of this book. There *are* a
lot of little ones, each one individually hardly worth a mention, but each one again etched in its way to a semblance of
perfection. (B)

Aaron Marc Stein. *Hangman's Row*. Doubleday/Crime Club, 1982,
181 pp., $10.95.
Lesley Egan. *Random Death*. Doubleday/Crime Club, 1982, 181
pp., $10.95.
Bernard St. James. *The Seven Dreamers*. Doubleday/Crime Club,
1982, 180 pp., $10.95.

One of the best days of the month, so far as I'm concerned,
is the day that the latest selection of mysteries from Double-
day's Crime Club comes in. Now, as most of you already probably know, this is no book club in the ordinary sense of the
term. The Crime Club has no dues (save the ever-increasing
price of the books), no membership rolls or requirements of any
kind, no free enticement offers--only books. Since 1928 or so,
they've been publishing mysteries and detective stories at the
rate of three or four a month--and there's no let-up in sight.
Generally speaking, the books published by the Crime Club
are prime examples of what's called "category publishing,"
aimed at a pre-set market. Most of them are gobbled up directly
by libraries. Few show up anywhere else but the specialized

mystery bookshop. There are few that reach the heights of ever being considered for an award of any kind, but there are few that are out-and-out losers, either.

I'm writing this in March, and last month's selections would have to be considered as pretty typical of what the Crime Club is producing today. There are two books by authors who have become long-time favorites, and one by a relative newcomer.

Aaron Marc Stein, for example, has been writing books, under three different names, for over forty-five years. He never seems to get much notice for his labors, but he can always be depended upon to tell a good, solid story. As Stein, writing about free-lance engineering expert Matt Erridge, his books tend more toward adventure than detection. As rumor has it, this is the way the publishers like it. Book after book, Erridge stumbles across mystery after mystery, and without half trying.

In *Hangman's Row* Erridge is in Amsterdam, helping a girl he first meets in the Van Gogh museum. Her boyfriend, it seems, is a decent artist himself. He is also a vociferous spokesman for various liberal causes, and he is in trouble with the police. An artistic array of protest effigies has been spoiled by the addition of a real body to the collection.

Although no more than a minor work at best, the story is enhanced considerably by the expertise Stein displays in local geography and customs. This is like a visit with an old friend --totally relaxed and comfortable leisure-time reading. (C plus)

Leslie Egan, on the other hand, usually has a lot more axes to grind in her books. Like Stein, she has been writing for many years now, and under several different pseudonyms. Her severest critics make much of her open support for various right-wing causes, and in one way or another her mystery novels, most of them police procedurals, usually reflect that same conservative point of view.

Random Death is one of her stories of the Glendale police force. All of the detectives are featured, but the cases of Vic Varallo and Delia Riordan are the ones followed most closely. The use of a policewoman as a main protagonist does not imply any feeling or support for ERA on Egan's part, however. Ms. Riordan deeply regrets her choice of career as it's worked out--no husband, no family, none of the things it is "most important for a woman to have."

Whether you agree or disagree, what makes Egan's books so alive is the strength of her convictions. As a suburb of Los Angeles, Glendale now seems to be under constant siege by criminal elements. Egan is simply unmatchable in terms of providing a voice of sympathy for the victims. Are the courts listening? (B plus)

As for the third book of the month, its author, Bernard St. James, has written one earlier novel featuring Chief Inspector Blanc of the Paris police. As yet, however, I'd be surprised if either were other than a brand new name to anyone but the most fervent mystery fancier.

The time is sometime in the early to mid-1800's, making *The Seven Sleepers* almost as much a historical novel as it is a detective story. Someone--a mesmerist, Blanc quickly deduces-- has slit the throats of everyone attending a small dinner party, while they were all sound asleep. Blanc's problem is not so much to discover who the guilty party is as it is to uncover the link between the victims which gives the culprit

his motive.
And here's where the history lesson comes in. As a mystery
novel, *The Seven Dreamers* seems badly paced and badly padded.
As historical fiction, it ends with a note of lofty idealism,
viewed with a necessary bit of perspective. The success of the
book, it would follow, would depend greatly on how strongly you
are in agreement. (B minus)

Chris Wiltz. *The Killing Circle*. Macmillan, 1981, 220 pp.,
    $11.95.

    I like private detective stories. Ordinarily, the first in
what promises to be a new private eye series is a matter for
rejoicing. Add a plot that begins with a set of missing books,
rare editions of William Blake, and the vividly moody background of New Orleans, and what we get this time is, well, a
book that just doesn't live up to its potential.
    The detective is named Neal Rafferty, and his biggest prob-
lem in life is that his father doesn't understand him. His
love life is in trouble too. He's quit the police force under
fire, and they don't like him too well either.
    The plot is nicely twisted, although sometimes to the point
where it becomes too heavily tangled in massive coincidence.
Rafferty meets a girl he can respond to, of course. The problem here is that the converse does not seem to be wholly true.
    What lets us down is the writing. The art of subtlety
seems utterly beyond Woltz's capabilities. Most of the story
she tells is stiff, formal, perfunctory, and placid.
    I wonder if that had anything to do with it. (C minus)*
    POSTSCRIPT: A small comment on expectations and how maybe
they influence the way you look at things. I read this book
all the way through thinking that Chris Wiltz was male, or
maybe not even thinking about it at all. Not until writing
the next-to-the-last paragraph did I look through the pro-
motional material Macmillan sent along with the book. That's
when I changed "he" to "she" and added the last line. I kept
the letter grade the same, however.

Shannon OCork. *End of the Line*. St. Martin's, 1981, 232 pp.,
    $10.95.

    This reads very much as it's supposed to, which is to say
like a story told by a liberated young lady working with some
caution and care in a world dominated by men. T.T. (Teresa
Tracy) Baldwin is an aspiring sports photographer for the *New
York Graphic*. She also solves mysteries.
    A murder occurs at a shark-hunting tournament, and it goes
without saying that the lesson learned from *Jaws* is not lost
on Shannon OCork before the case is finally wrapped up. There
are also some missing diamonds and an antagonistic small-town
cop solidly in a rich man's pocket.
    As a mystery, the story is sometimes a puzzler in more ways
than one. Obvious questions (to the reader, at least) are
never asked, apparently never even thought of, until at length
T.T. reveals she already knew the answers, far earlier than she
ever let on.
    From another point of view, the broken style T.T. persists

in using in telling her own story adds immediacy to the first part of the story, and a considerable amount of fast, page-turning excitement to the finale. In between, it simply becomes hard to read.

Other than T.T., who is bright, smart-alecky, and certain to get ahead, most of the remaining characters are straight from summer stock. The ending *is* worth waiting for, however. (B minus)

Simon Brett. *Situation Tragedy*. Scribner's, 1981, 170 pp., $9.95.

In case you've never come across one of these mystery adventures of actor-sleuth Charles Paris before, be forewarned: there will be times when you will be convinced that if there is any detection going on it is definitely taking second place to Simon Brett's witty, caustic commentary on the world of show business, British style.

In this, his seventh case, Paris tackles the world of commercial television. Somewhat to his own surprise, he has a bit part in a new sitcom. It's a continuing part, at least--but so's the series of fatal "accidents" that begin to plague the show, and even before the first episode is ever aired!

Also be forewarned that Charles Paris is something of a tosspot and a womanizer, but he is certanly also one not to be overly impressed with the glamour of show-biz. There are also a couple of digs at the peculiarities of some mystery collectors. (Nobody who doesn't deserve it!)

The ending is tragic, scarcely believable, and yet, mostly a fitting one. (B)*

Warren Murphy. *Dying Space*. Pinnacle, 1982, 196 pp., $2.25.

Here is the forty-seventh in the continuing adventures of Remo Williams, aka "The Destroyer." And right here this probably tells you all that you want to know about this book. Either you've bought and read it already, or you have absolutely no intention of doing either one. Go on to the next review.

As for me, well, I'm somewhere in the middle. I think I have them all, but I also think I've read something like every seventeenth one. And only somebody who's read them all could say for sure, but there must be hills and valleys, noticeable ups and downs within the series itself. So I don't know, but I think this is a valley.

For openers, this one has a lady astrophysicist with a yen for booze and Italian soccer teams. It has a mysterious, advanced computer of her own design, and somebody (something?) named Mr. Gordons, who is a deadly robot and an implacable enemy of Remo and his Korean mentor, Chiun. There is also, almost incidentally, a Russian plot to poison the moon.

Apparently Mr. Gordons has been around before. He will also most assuredly be around again, as once again (WARNING: you may not want to know this ahead of time) he manages to escape total dismantlement and/or destruction.

Otherwise, nothing much seems to happen.

I laughed a lot, though. (To put that statement into

proper perspective, I was *supposed* to.)
    I wonder why former co-author Richard Sapir no longer wants credit for writing these things? (C minus)

James Ellroy. *Brown's Requiem*. Avon, 1981, 256 pp., $2.50.

    It took me a while to track this book down--Avon's distribution system did not seem to reach the Northeast too effectively for a while last fall--but I'm glad I finally did. In recent months Avon has been doing some of the best mysteries to be published in paperback, particularly in the realm of first edition originals, and this is one of them.
    I'm almost tempted to say it's also a private eye story for people who hate private eye stories, but there are also some people whom I'm sure would rather die than admit to liking the things, even if they did, and so I won't.
    Fritz Brown is the P.I., and his client is a crazy caddy named Fat Dog who flashes hundred-dollar bills and wants Brown to keep an eye on his sister, an aspiring cello player living with an elderly Jew named Kupferman who is now in the fur business.
    In a way, the whole book is just as slightly looney as this may sound, which is part of its cockeyed charm. What is meant for dialogue often consists of long, one-sided monologues, and if you let it it could easily drive you nuts. Ellroy's version of Los Angeles is a sad, seedy one, described by someone who knows, brightened only by the green oases of its many available golf courses.
    Brown's life story, a lonely one, whether he admits it or not, naturally becomes interwoven with the one he gradually unravels and inexorably ties back together.
    Like a "literary" novel of more recognizable form, bits of philosophy and the deeper implication of things like the perquisites of power and the demands of those who pursue it, are integral ingredients of the story Ellroy tells, and he takes the time and space to tell it well.
    What I find strange, however, is how much more I seem to be appreciating the book now--two weeks later--than I remember that I did while I was actually reading it. I don't want to push the musical comparison too greatly, but the fact remains--profane as it may seem at times, this book sings. (A minus)

Robert B. Parker. *Ceremony*. Delacorte/Lawrence, 1982, 182 pp., $12.95.

    In a number of ways, we have gone through cases like this one before. Spenser is still Boston's premier private eye, but taking a first look at his latest adventure it may appear that he's dangerously on the edge of repeating himself once too often.
    When he's not confronting various social issues like radical feminism the only way he can--head on--Spenser has always been concerned with the welfare of adolescent youth and parents who can't seem to cope, or don't seem to care.
    In *Early Autumn*, which was two books ago, now, Spenser took a young boy under his wing and inspired and bullied him by example into starting to care about his life. In *Ceremony*

he switches direction 180 degrees and tries to rescue a teen-
aged girl, an unhappy high school dropout, from a life in the
Combat Zone. This, of course, as everyone probably knows, is.
Boston's notorious "everything goes" downtown district.

And as he always does, Spenser has a solution, but this
time it's hardly one designed to please social workers of any
kind. In a definite sense, that it's right doesn't necessarily
make it right.

If this doesn't sound like your typical private-eye novel,
there's no reason it should. That's not the kind Parker writes,
and maybe it's about time some of his detractors accepted it.
There are crimes involved, to be sure, including one rather
sordid scandal that comes to light. Spenser gives no quarter
when it comes to saving April Kyle, even against her will.
Before it's over, there's violence enough to satisfy the most
action-starved fanatic.

The characters still come first, however. Whether you
agree with the final outcome or not, Robert B. Parker has taken
some entirely human problems and solved them with just enough
of a reverse twist to keep both the intellect and emotional
adrenelin running finely along in high gear.

Brinksmanship or not, there's not much more we can ask from
a book. (A)*

Stella Allan. *An Inside Job*. Avon, 1980, 224 pp., $2.25
(first published in 1978).

Most of the mainstream critics who commented on the recent
movie "Body Heat" compared it, not illogically, to the works of
James M. Cain. Those of us in the know (as we're prone to say)
will also say that here was the closest adaptation of an old
Gold Medal paperback novel that's ever been made. Consider the
theme: an unwary male victim is caught up in the temptations of
a beautiful woman's lush afterglow, sinking him deeper and
deeper into a never-ending web of crime and deceit. "Raiders
of the Lost Ark" notwithstanding, "Body Heat" certainly got my
vote for the movie of the year. It simply sizzled.

But back to the tale at hand. This nifty little novel of
murder and retribution neatly reverses the theme of all those
sultry paperback novels of the 50's. This time around a fem-
inist it is, rising to the top of the business world, who finds
herself putty in the hands of her best friend's husband.

Times have changed, and the roles have been reversed. The
ensuing death of Sheila Pettit's employer and long-time mentor
causes her no feeling of sorrow or regret.

And this could be the greatest problem you will find with
this book. None of the people involved could be described as
even half-way appealing. The futures they cut out for themselves no one could possibly conclude are other than what they
most richly deserve.

As I'm sure I've said before, the British seem to do *this*
kind of story better than anyone else. (B minus)

Verdicts

More Reviews

Robert B. Parker. *Ceremony*. Delecorte Press, 1982, 182 pp., $12.95.

Two appearances ago, Spenser, Robert B. Parker's hero, undertook the salvation of a teenaged boy's character and personality. In Parker's new book, *Ceremony*, Spenser once again determines the future of a youngster, April Kyle, runaway and prostitute. Like her predecessor, Paul Giacomin, April is irritating, pitiful, stubborn, confused, and totally disengaged from any meaningful relationship with her family. Readers may not like April much, but they may well recognize her and the forces, within and without, which formed her. Spenser's decisions on April's behalf are surely going to be unsettling for many readers, but those decisions are taken only after full consultation with April herself as well as with the remarkable, reliable Susan Silverman. And not without a great deal of serious, somewhat uncomfortable thought by Spenser himself.

Spenser *can* think, and he can feel, abilities that put him in the major leagues of fictional private eyes. When--as here --Spenser plays God, he does it carefully and introspectively, unlike Poirot, who talks constantly about his brain power but shares few "thoughts in process" with his readers. Spenser talks his way through his cases, sharing both certainties and doubts with his readers. This device is not at all new, as fans well know, but Parker handles it better with each novel, and it accounts for a good deal of the books' appeal.

In many ways, Spenser's main cohorts represent the two sides of his personality. Susan underscores and nourishes his thoughtfulness and his capacity to empathize. Hawk, his black ex-boxer and strong-arm friend, very effectively supports Spenser the man of action, the product of the Hemingway code who both honors and questions that code. The strength of these important supporting players lies in the fact that Parker convinces readers that both Susan and Hawk have vigorous lives of their own; they are more than puppets taken occasionally from their racks to fill a gap in a Spenser story. It is Susan, in fact, who suggests to April's unappetizing parents that Spenser locate their runaway daughter. April has been one of Susan's student referrals at the high school in which she works as a counselor. As so often happens, Spenser goes well beyond his contracted responsibility.

Other familiar Parker/Spenser ingredients are also present

--restaurants, menus, running, Boston-area geography, wines, music--the whole slate. These details do lend verisimilitude and do deepen Spenser's characterization a bit as they are meant to do, but the best deepening device is Spenser talking-- to Susan, to Hawk (though these conversations are highly styl- ized and elliptical), and to us, the readers. There's one point, however, where Parker flubs the willing suspension of disbelief: it is impossible that Susan Silverman cannot manage a simple job of parallel parking. I simply don't believe it! (Jane S. Bakerman)

Dick Francis. *Twice Shy*. G.P. Putnam's Sons, 1982, 307 pp.

In *Twice Shy*, the always readable, always interesting Dick Francis takes a long chance; he breaks his story in the middle, in effect blending two short novels into one long one. The book begins with physics teacher Jonathan Derry's encounter with a workable betting system, computers, and a deadly family of gamblers who want that system. Fourteen years later, William Derry, Jonathan's much younger brother, manager of a wealthy American's fine race horses, takes up the battle when the most dangerous of the hoods attacks him in search of vengeance and easy money. Francis manages the break and the shift handily; the book works, but there is one major problem.

While Jonathan Derry's personality is well and carefully established--he is one of Francis' most interesting characters --the portrait seems truncated because Part I itself is un- resolved; it just stops. William's personality seems far less well-established, and the denouement of Part II, William's seg- ment, is also abrupt and arbitrary. In a sense, these un- resolved conclusions may be taken as lifelike, but literary realism demands a bit more polishing, a bit more rounding off.

However, Francis' minor characters in *Twice Shy* are among the very best he's produced. Sarah, Jonathan's unhappy, un- sympathetic wife, constrasts effectively with Cassie, William's poised, self-possessed lover. Their friend, Bananas Frisby, pub-keeper, restaurateur, and bitter philosopher, is whole and persuasive. He serves as a contrast to the intriguing Ted Pitts, Jonathan's computer-genius friend who is not so simple a personality as he first seems. Even the brief appearance of Ruth Quigly, graduate student entranced with computers, im- patient with her own youthfulness, is splendid; and alert, aged Mrs. O'Rorke is a gem. These solid portraits serve and strengthen the comparison-contrast pattern of the plot, for a major point of interest is the similarities and differences in the ways the Derry brothers confront danger, violence, and death. This pattern and the vivid minor characters combine with Francis' usual mastery of technical detail and action to produce a plot stronger than its protagonists.

Twice Shy is a good book, and though the Derry brothers may be a shade disappointing, they are well worth meeting. By and large, Francis wins his risky bet. (Jane S. Bakerman)

Rick Boyer. *Billingsgate Shoal*. Houghton Mifflin, 1982, 272 pp., $11.95.

Boyer's protagonist is Doc Adams, an oral surgeon going

through that middle-aged questioning of life; Doc has been taking a good, hard look, and, like the rest of us, he finds it
routinely humdrum. He doesn't like what he sees. But if he
only knew, he'd like what he sees one morning at 5:00 a.m.
through his binoculars even less. He sees a boat beached on
Billingsgate Shoal. This simple observation becomes the first
link in a chain of murder, smuggling, and hidden treasure--all
the ingredients for a real suspense-mystery tour de force.
    And a tour de force it is.
    The boat that Doc spies stranded intentionally on the shoal
is later involved in the death of a young man (for which Doc
feels he is indirectly responsible). Adams sets out to find
this mystery ship. He manages to snap several photographs of
the ship before it unaccountably drops from sight. A trip to
the Coast Guard office in Boston turns up a faked carpenter's
certificate. Doc's investigative digging leads him to a fish-
erman's bar in Gloucester, where he gets embroiled in a dispute
not of his making; he delves into illegal reconstruction and
alterations of boats in a dingy, beercan-strewn shipyard; he
discovers the involvement of a man reported dead for several
years; he follows the trail to a vanished treasure hunter and
his unhappy wife.
    Boyer's attention to detail is acute, but it never detracts
from the pace of the story itself. His description of Doc's
solo cruise by sailboat from Wellfleet to Plymouth is very well
done and extremely realistic. The conclusion of *Billingsgate
Shoal* is full of action and suspense galore, with an amusing
episode that plays on a bit of local history concerning the
purchase of property by the "Moonies."
    Boyer has woven a tight fabric that does manage to include
some of the local restaurants, landmarks, and the like in the
name-dropping manner of Robert B. Parker, but one never feels
that the local color is more important than the story itself.
    Doc Adams, on the other hand, has unusual skills for an
oral surgeon. He is very adept at Karate and judo and tends
to be singularly without fear. In the course of the tale he
manages to take out three professional thugs with an ease that
somehow feels overdone.   •
    This aside, *Billingsgate Shoal* should provide enough plot
twists and turns to keep you interested and abreast of Doc
Adams and his relentless pursuit of the solution to the mystery. (Alan S. Mosier)

Anne Morice. *Hollow Vengeance.* St. Martin's Press, 1982,
    173 pp., $10.95.

    The latest Morice novel, starring as usual actress/amateur
sleuth Tessa Crichton, has several characteristics that have
become Morice trademarks. As in other novels, Tessa is visit-
ing an old friend and finds a disturbing atmosphere of brittle
tempers. Contributing to a familiar theme is the fact that
largely responsible for the disgruntlement is a new neighbor's
attempt to make drastic changes in the physical environment.
There are fully drawn young people, and, as in other Morice
novels, some are wonderful and some are horrible. Also as
usual, Tessa bumbles around being impulsive through most of the
novel but finally pulls all the loose ends together herself to
solve the crimes.

The despicable character who is the obvious target for murder is Mrs. Trelawney. This form of her name is the only one given, and it is an ironic pun since her every intention seems to be to uproot the trees and run fences through the lawns. She is wealthy, insensitive, and unfriendly. With youthful disregard for danger, Marcus Carrington, son of Tessa's friend and host Elsa, loudly proclaims to the world at large that he will one day murder the nasty new neighbor, Mrs. Trelawney. Elsa complicates the matter by unwittingly implicating Marc for Mrs. Trelawney's murder by telling a fib for a wholly unrelated purpose. Tessa assumes the responsibility for vindicating Marc while finding the explanation for all of the odd events. Other neighbors have prominent parts and, with the Carringtons, provide a closed circle of suspects. Tessa determines the real personalities behind their appearances.

A foil introduced late in the book draws attention to the wrong parties, as it is meant to do, but the action could not have been inspired as Tessa explains it. Otherwise, Tessa deduces quite reasonable motives, methods, and opportunities. Each character's part in the drama falls in place with Tessa's typical end-of-the book speech to regulars Robin (her husband), Toby (her cousin), and their host.

Hollow Vengeance is another charmer from Anne Morice. (Martha Alderson)

Max Collins. *Scratch Fever*. Pinnacle, 1982, $1.95.

Max Collins' tough guy/ex-bank robber Nolan is back in what may be the last of his action-filled exploits. The series may be discontinued because of a lawsuit which claims name infringement over the similarity between Don Pendleton's Bolan and the Collins character.

Even without such controversy, this Nolan story is a delight, combining aspects of the rock mystique and comic fandom with the crime novel. Nolan's young comic-loving friend Jon is also the keyboard man for a rock group, The Nodes. While playing a gig, Jon spots his and Nolan's most recent adversary, the lovely and double-dealing Julie who tried to kill them following a recent bank heist.

Julie also spots Jon, gets a tough accomplice to kidnap him, and hires hit men from Chicago to kill Nolan. But Nolan's sense of danger is too acute. He's over fifty, still alive in a violent business, and he realizes that he must "eliminate" Julie and rescue his partner.

A Nolan book is always a rewarding reading experience. Collins, who writes the comic Dick Tracy, has a knack for superb characterization and fast-paced action. In a world in which homogenized TV monopolizes entertainment, Nolan's realistic fictional world is quite refreshing.

Collins is quite adept at writing compelling dialogue and structuring unexpected plot twists. *Scratch Fever* is crime writing at its most effective, and, as a bonus, it just might be the first book to incorporate new wave music into the crime genre. (Jim Traylor)

Julian Symons. *Great Detectives*. Abrams, 1981, 144 pp., $18.50 (illustrated by Tom Adams).

Symons states in his introduction that he was asked to
write biographies of the Great Detectives--Holmes, Miss Marple,
Nero Wolfe, Ellery Queen, Maigret, Poirot, and Philip Marlowe.
He decided to embellish them a bit, hence the subtitle "Seven
Original Investigations."

As in any Abrams book, the production is beautiful--nicely
bound, plentifully illustrated, and of high quality throughout.
The artist states that he attempted to illustrate with "period
pieces" in keeping with the stories. He has succeeded with the
period, though there will probably be many complaints about the
representations of favorite detectives. I for one can't stand
his portrayal of Wolfe.

Symons takes an interesting approach to each of the detectives: Holmes solves a case in retirement; the Vicar of St.
Mary Mead tells about Miss Marple (and the village); Symons
"interviews" Archie (an old Archie). Then there's an interview
with the "real" detective who was the model for Marlowe, and
"biographies with a twist" take care of the others.

A beautiful, intriguing book--BUT. I must confess I came
away uneasy. A large part of my dis-ease was engendered by
Symons' interview with Archie in which he has Archie refer to
himself as "doddering." Ultimately, Symons fails because he
has attempted to reduce heroic figures to mere mortal status.
(Linda Toole)

Bob Reiss. *Summer Fires*. Pocket Books, 1980, 311 pp., $2.75
(originally published by Simon & Schuster in 1980).

Summer Fires, Reiss's first novel, tells the story of pov-
erty lawyer Miles Bradshaw's search for the arsonist-murderer
responsible for the death of a youth caught in a South Bronx
tenement fire. Bradshaw, a tenement resident himself, is more
motivated than many would be to seek out the arsonist, for he
is guilty of accidentally starting a fire which caused the
death of his own family.

Bradshaw soon finds that there has been a pattern of fires,
or "torchings," all clustered in the South Bronx area. The
usual motive for such a pattern of arson is the payment of in-
surance to the absentee landlords, who hire youth gangs to
torch their buildings. But Bradshaw discovers that this pattern is different--much more serious, with a much more lucra-
tive payoff. Much of the mystery revolves around a science
fiction-like, gleaming metal tower constructed inside one of
the buildings in the area. To learn the secret of the build-
ing, Bradshaw employs sort of a "Fort Apache, Bronx Irregulars"
group--a Puerto Rican youth gang called the Latin Kings. His
search also involves him with his next door neighbor, a strik-
ingly beautiful Latin woman.

Part detective story, part intrigue story, part whydunit,
and part adventure, *Summer Fires* is yet simple and chillingly
written. There is something akin to the tone of a horror story
in Reiss's coolly impersonal and unemotional prose. Characters
and physical events are described sparsely, but quite originally.
I was mildly surprised to see within the first ten pages that a
sinister Oriental would be involved. In fact, though, the book
would have been better and tighter as a detective story had it
followed Bradshaw's actions alone, without shifting the narrative between him and the villain. Last but not least, the

motive for the fires and the villain's machinations is intended
to be a surprise; it would be much more surprising if the comments of the book's editor did not give it away. If you buy
the book, try not to read the back cover. (Greg Goode)

Roy Harley Lewis. *A Cracking of Spines*. St. Martin's Press,
1982, 207 pp., $10.95.

British bibliophile and bookseller Roy Lewis has written an
engaging thriller about Matthew Coll, a British intelligence
agent who buys a bookstore in the country to lead a quieter and
less dangerous life. He is promptly hired by the Antiquarian
Booksellers Association to solve a series of thefts of old and
valuable books. There is a smashing portrait of a beautiful
and intelligent lady of the manor who is knowledgeable about
books and doesn't consider her stodgy husband too much of a
hindrance to her response to ex-agent Matthew Coll's infatua-
tion. There are some vicious thugs, a girlfriend who quickly
becomes an ex-girlfriend when Coll meets Lady Caroline, a high-
speed pursuit, some brutal fights, and a touching death scene
where the master villain (who is about as engaging as Coll and
the narrative) expires bloodily but heroically.
Lewis's writing about old books is as infectious as Jonathan
Gash's writing about antiques, but the women are something more
than birds and Coll is a more sympathetic bloke than macho,
super-stud Lovejoy. Characterization, although it is fairly
basic, is less adolescent in Lewis's romance than it is in
Gash's. Not a volume for the ages, but in an age where people
understand that having a little obsession on the side is very
healthy, the reader can enjoy the author's fantasies and if
they coincide with his own imagine that he is having a satis-
fying time. In short, for the dedicated bibliophile and the
aficionado of fast, undemanding reads. (Walter Albert)

William Marshall. *Sci Fi*. Rinehart, 1981.

Number six in the chronicle of the antics of the frantic,
often comical cops at the Yellowthread Street precinct in Hong
Kong. Dyed-in-the-wool science-fiction fans will be put off by
the title, nit-picking grammatical types will frown at the
missing hyphen, and fans of the series will probably find this
to be an average outing for the boys.
A character in a space-man outfit roams the corridors of
the Empress of India Hotel, cremating people with his ray gun
and posing the threat of a holocaust in which not only the
hotel but much of adjacent Hong Kong might go up in flames.
The "sci fi" is not only the make-believe spaceman but the
assorted costumed characters attending the annual All-Asia
Science Fiction and Horror Movie Festival. There is funny
movie talk by some enterprising Asian producers about junky
science fiction epics, the threat of a Japanese Mafia, a series
of muggings in a parking garage performed by a man in a dis-
appearing van, and a continuing attempt by Senior Detective
Inspector Christopher O'Yee to get passes to the festival film
event to which he, in a moment of great weakness, has promised
to take his wife, children, and assorted friends.

(Continued on page 29)

The Documents
In the Case

Letters

From Jim Traylor, 5130 Thistle Road; Smyrna, GA   30080:
   Did I say that I enjoyed Walter Albert's "Reel Murders"?
Excellent commentary! For me, the enjoyment of reading a mystery story is enhanced by the visual experience. Hence my love
for mystery movies. (I tend to slot them in my mind as "murder
mysteries" and I love both the tricky and the hard-boiled.)
Then, too, hearing the old radio mysteries is quite an experience. The local radio in Atlanta is doing a series called
"Let's Watch the Radio" which includes a number of mysteries
and/or police shows such as *Dragnet, Boston Blackie, Gangbust-
ers, Suspense,* and others. All are interesting for the genre
and usually fun to experience or (for some of us) to re-
experience.
   [...] Oh, one query: I'm trying to locate a copy (xerox is
okay) of Carroll John Daly's "'The Flame' and Race Williams,"
Black Mask, August 1931 (Part 3 of a three-part serial). Can
anyone of our number help?

From Charles Shibuk, 2084 Bronx Park East, Bronx, NY   10462:
   I was extremely interested to see Walter Albert's new col-
umn, "Reel Murders," and shall look forward to future install-
ments.
   I might also add that Professor Albert is not the only per-
son who believes in the supremacy of silent films over talkies.
   Unfortunately, I noted several errors in this column.
   The 1919 serial films by Fritz Lang (which I personally
found to be disappointing) are correctly titled *The Spiders*
(*Die Spinnen*).
   Spies (*Spione*)--not *The Spies*--is a 1928 Lang film.
   Lang's *You Only Live Once* obviously shares much thematic
material with *Thieves Like Us,* but it is technically incorrect
to call the latter a remake of the former.
   You Only Live Once is based on a screen original by Graham
Baker and Gene Towne.
   Thieves Like Us is based on the novel of the same title by
Edward Anderson which was published in 1937--the same year that
You Only Live Once was released.
   Incidentally, the first film version of the novel *Thieves
Like Us* was *They Live by Night,* which was released in 1949 and
marked Nicholas Ray's directorial debut.
   Bob Adey has my sympathy because he doesn't have a copy of
Lucinda in his legendary collection. I don't either, but at

least I've read it.

From David J. Wilf, 3701 Conshohocken Ave. #307, Phila., PA:
[*David is a new subscriber.*] I was extremely disappointed
with the issue you just mailed me (vol. 6, no. 2). If that had
been the issue that introduced me to your magazine I never
would have subscribed. My big complaint is that in a fifty
page issue you have filled up *eleven* of them (more than twenty
percent of the issue) with movie reviews. I for one want to
read about books, authors, reviews, etc.--not movie reviews.
The reviews of the current movies I can, and have, read in the
daily newspapers and *Time*--at least three reviews of each. The
reviews of the old, old movies--so what--we can't see them
anyhow.
     In the present issue of *The Armchair Detective* (vol. 15,
no. 1), out of ninety-six pages they have devoted *three* pages to
both movies and TV. Please either drop the movie reviews alto-
gether, or allow them no more than one or two pages per issue.

From Linda Toole, 40 Hermitage Rd., Rochester, NY 14617:
     Your canvas of potential subscribers had at least one
strange offshoot. I received a letter from someone in Penn-
sylvania who saw my letter in the sample you sent out. He
stated that he had long corresponded with a neighbor of mine
who had never answered his last letter. He then proceeded to
give me the lowdown on the less savory facets of this man's
character. The kicker is that the man had been dead at least
five years! Thanks to your comments in 6:1 I now know how he
got my address. [*Just another of the countless benefits of
subscribing to TMF. Have you gotten any anonymous phone calls
yet?*]
     I heartily second your suggestion to Louise Gagnon re tapes
of the Nero Wolfe radio shows. Good, bad, or indifferent (the
shows--not the tapes), I would be interested in purchasing a
set--or even one show. [*One of our Canadian brethren, whose
name I will withhold to keep him from being swamped with plead-
ing letters, was so generous as to make and send me a tape of
the program based on "Before I Die." It was surprisingly
faithful to the story and quite entertaining to listen to. I
envy those who got to listen to all of the broadcasts. The
radio program was several orders of magnitude better than
either the TV series or the TV movie. Mavor Moore played Wolfe
and Don Francks was Archie. Send me a buck to cover postage,
and I'll mail the tape up to you for you to duplicate. Same
offer goes for any other TMFers who would like to make a copy,
but you'll have to get in line.*]
     I must disagree with Greg Goode. I do not like the slick
cover for several reasons. One is a personal preference for
the dull paper; another is that the letters on the back page
are hard to read due to glare and smudging. [*No slick cover
this time--see what power you have?*] As long as I'm speaking
about the magazine--WHAT IN THE WORLD HAPPENED TO THE "DEPART-
MENT HEADINGS"? [*What happened to the department heads is
this. They were done up a couple of years ago when I had access to clip books and certain type fonts. When I added Walter's "Reel Murders" as a new feature, I no longer had access
to clip books and I couldn't duplicate the type face, so I just
dropped all the art and reset all the department heads. I did
it to be consistent, but the truth of the matter is that I was*]

*getting a bit bored with that familiar old artwork. (I put it
together myself, so I can say that without risk of offending
anyone.)]*

Hope there will be more on comic heroes from Mr. Blom. His
first article was great. And speaking of more, thank God "Reel
Murders" is going to be a regular. It's always a pleasure to
read something from a person who is both knowledgeable and en-
amored. Keep it up, Walter!

Thanks for the tip on *Huntress*. I've long been a fan of
the Avengers (original), and this magazine is a delight. I'm
looking forward to future issues.

Are there any Sherlockians in our midst? If so, I have a
favor to ask. I just purchased (at a ridiculously small price)
three volumes of a set of Holmes entitled "The Sherlock Holmes
Series," published by Harper and Brothers in 1904. The first
volume contains two novels, the second and third are collec-
tions of short stories. The volumes are illustrated (Paget,
Carelton, etc.) and the frontispiece of volume one is a picture
of Doyle. Under the picture is a two-line inscription: "Yours
faithfully, A. Conan Doyle." I think this is probably a photo
reproduction, but does anyone know for sure?

From Jim Goodrich, 5 Ulster Road, New Paltz, NY 12561:

K. Arne Blom's opinion of Al Williamson's Secret Agent X9
as "a bleak and ridiculous copy of James Bond" is strictly his
own. I consider the strip brilliant and fascinating; I believe
most fellow strip fans do likewise. What, by the by, is wrong
with being "surrounded with girls with nice hips and big tits"?
Bad hips and small boobs are preferable? Buz Sawyer was similar to Captain Easy? The characters certainly weren't, in my
unhumble opinion. Re Steve Roper and Mike Nomad, Allen (not
Allan) Saunders lets son John do the writing. At least I
learned more about Buck Ryan from Arne, and anyone who enjoys
Fearless Fosdick can't be all bad!

Bob Sampson does his usual highly professional job on "The
Professionals." Thanks, Bob. Merci, too, Marv, for your con-
sistently interesting contribs in whatever zine they appear.

One of your Stout spies has sans doute informed you that
Brownstone House of Nero Wolfe, Darby, will be pubbed by Little,
Brown this month at $13.00.

From Greg Goode, 50 Washburn Park, Rochester, NY 14620:

Barry Van Tilburg mentions movies in 6:2, in which you also
have *two* film columns, so perhaps I can comment on some films.

Lee Horsley might have been slick and pretty as Archie
Goodwin, but he's rough and rugged as Talon the Barbarian in
the recently released movie *The Sword and the Sorcerer.* Enough
publicity had been given about *Conan* (which was 4-5 years in
the making) that Horsley's movie was probably made quickly to
capitalize on the enthusiasm. And so that not too many could
call S&S a *Conan* ripoff, S&S was released before *Conan.* The
plots, characters, and even many of the images and sequences
in the two films are quite similar.

The Blade Runner and *Firefox,* both book adaptations, will
soon be released this summer, along with Steve Martin's nos-
talgic *Dead Men Don't Wear Plaid,* which, I have heard, has
footage from some Bogart, Ladd, and Powell P.I. films. I'm
looking forward to seeing *Wrong Is Right* tonight; it is also
an adaptation of Charles McCarry's *The Better Angels.*

I wasn't able to hear it, but I heard about it--Donald E. Westlake was a guest on *The Larry King Show*, on about 280 stations around the country, on the A.M. (EST) of 14 May.

I subscribe to *Mystery News*, but, aside from the interviews they sometimes have, there is not much book news that tells more than the sum of reading (i) NYTBR, TMF, TPP, TAD, and (ii) scouring the local bookstore. But I suppose that one publication containing all of that is much easier to peruse. *Mystery News* ought, I think, to carry (more) information on the publication of secondary sources.

From Jean & Walter Shine, 122 Lakeshore Dr., N. Palm Beach, FL:
In your next issue, among the new publications, you might want to include the forthcoming (by then already out) from Frederick Ungar Publishing Co.: Professor David Geherin's *John D. MacDonald*, the first book-length analysis of JDM's writings (200 pp., $11.95 cloth, $6.95 paper). Haven't seen it yet but will keep you in touch when it arrives here. Think p. 44 of vol. 6, no. 2, has misprint, in Floyd's review of JDM's *Red* and *Orange* books. Third paragraph reference to Red should be to Orange--or at least that's how we read it. Also think his Gruber review contradicts the comments in the preceding one on those books. [*It's not a misprint; that's the way Frank wrote it. Care to respond, Frank?*]

From Barry Van Tilburg, 4380 67th Ave., N., Pinellas Park, FL:
I have decided to do the Paperback series. [*The first installment will appear in the next TMF.*] In all the reference books I have read no one to date has given spies of fiction their due. Nick Carter for some reason has been deleted from almost every reference volume so far, yet it is the best selling fiction spy series of all time.

Espionage books are very intricate. It's no longer whodunit but who is doing what to whom? Is your boss really your boss or an enemy? Is your partner really your partner? Is an enemy really an enemy? Is a dead man really dead? There are more twists to a spy story than any other story I have ever read, and that is what makes it for me.

From Bill Crider, 4206 Ninth Street, Brownwood, TX 76801:
A lesser person than myself might take umbrage at K. Arne Blom's passing reference to the "stupid and idiotic Nick Carter tradition." I mean, why "stupid *and* idiotic"? Couldn't he have settled for just plain "stupid"? Or just plain "idiotic"? Then there's Steve Lewis's review, in which he calls my all-time favorite Nick Carter book "drivel." I figured I had a handle on "stupid and idiotic." "Drivel," well, I decided to look that one up. According to my dictionary, it means "silly, foolish, childish talk; twaddle." Of course, I've heard the phrase, "driveling idiot." I begin to suspect that Blom and Lewis are in cahoots. But what the heck, I forgive them. When they come grovelling to me for autographs, though, they can forget it.

I want to put in a good word for Charles Shibuk's recommendation of Howard Rigsby's *Lucinda*. Charlie and I usually don't read the same stuff (or at least he doesn't usually admit reading it), but we certainly agree on *Lucinda*. It's too bad that his wish for its immediate reprinting probably won't be carried out, and the book is pretty hard to find in its original Gold

Medal edition--one reason may be that neither the author's name nor the title appears on the spine. You've got to look at the cover.

From David Wilkerson, Rt. 1, Box 5, Days Creek, OR 97429:
You might be interested in a series (I think) of books by David Smith about a young white guy and an old African man working on cases in modern Africa. I have only read one and it was from the library, but it was great. The book I read was published in the last year or so. It was the second or third of a series, I believe. I'm looking for them all.
I have also discovered the Con Madden and Daniel Glower books by Maurice Walsh. I have *Nine Strings to Your Bow* and cannot wait to get the Hubin I have ordered to see which others were published. Most likely you were aware of these authors, but you have given me such pleasure in *The Mystery Fancier* that I thought I would bring them up. Smith's books and to a lesser degree the Maurice Walsh books both have the humor, characterization, and humanness that is Nero Wolfe and Archie.
[I must confess to being unfamiliar with both of the authors you speak of. The only David Smith listed in Hubin's Biblio-graphy is David MacLeod Smith, whose books are listed under his pseudonym, David Mariner. Could he be the one? Hubin lists these titles: The Beaufort Dossier *(Hale, 1973; Zebra, 1974);* The Chatham Rats *(Hale, 1969) [published in the U.S. as* Operation Scorpio *(Pinnacle, 1975)];* Devil's Bread *(Hale, 1969) [published in the U.S. as* The Yaroslav Incident *(Zebra, 1974)];* A Shackleton Called Sheila *(Hale, 1970) [published in the U.S. as* Countdown 1000 *(Pinnacle, 1974)]; and* Symbol of Vengeance *(Hale, 1975). Naturally, any titles published after 1975 would not appear in Al's Bibliography.]*
[As for the Maurice Walsh books, Hubin only lists two: Nine Strings to Your Bow *(Lippincott, 1945), which you mention, appears to have been published by Chambers in England earlier that same year under the title* The Man in Brown. *The other is* Danger Under the Moon *(Chambers, 1956; Lippincott, 1957). You write as though Walsh did a series featuring Con Madden and Daniel Glower; does anyone know whether these characters figured in* Danger Under the Moon? *Al gives Walsh's birth year as 1879, so it is unlikely that he wrote anything after Al's 1975 cutoff date; is it possible that Al missed any earlier books?]*

From Ev Bleiler, still hiding out in the New Jersey jungles:
Shame on you! You left a paragraph out of my article!
[Gulp!]
After "hangs dying" *[the last words on p. 9]* and before "In an unsigned preface" *[the first words on p. 10]* should go

Back in England Floss's plans for the inheritance also collapse. Mugginson and O'Mazem learn of the conspiracy and rescue Able Poordevil after a sea chase in Liverpool harbor. Crime is punished and virtue is rewarded. *[Mea, as usual, culpa.]*

I wouldn't be buying your proposed reissue of the Preview and Volume One of TMF (since I already have them) and probably should keep my mouth shut. But I think it is an excellent idea to reprint. Mystery material is library-chic right now, and the venture should be viable, as well as editorially worth while.